Fig

A Short Story Cycle

Dael Allison

PUNCHER & WATTMANN

First published in 2026
Published by Puncher & Wattmann
PO Box 279
Waratah NSW 2298

info@puncherandwattmann.com

A catalogue record for this book is available from The National Library of Australia.

ISBN 9781923099852

Cover image by Dael Allison

Cover design by David Musgrave and Pippa Haughton

Printed by Lightning Source International

Contents

To my family, always.
To the first nations guardians of the *Coquun*/Hunter River region.
To all those who rise with Rising Tide: risingtide.org.au

01: 1937 Silksworth

Qui's role is to stay dead. He lies motionless on the ship's cold deck, a young Chinese man on his back, limbs splayed. If he moves even a finger, he will betray the pact with *Biǎojiě*, who protects him now by submitting to that insane Japanese *wōkòu*.

His head cants to the side and his eyes are shut. If he opened them, he would see the source of the sounds that batter in his brain. The Japanese ship's officer viciously beating a seaman. That seaman is his cousin.

It is nearly dark. A wet sea mist creeps along the pier where the ship is moored, blurring the harsh yellow of the high dock lights.

Biǎojiě grunts at another blow.

Qui feels each kick, his own thin body a network of pain from the officer's frenzied attack, before he turned on *Biǎojiě*. His head still rings from the punch that lifted him off his feet and threw him backwards, his head smashing against the deck..He probes a broken molar with his tongue. Fights against gagging as blood trickles down his throat.

Not a quiver.

He knows the officer's rage goes beyond retribution for discovering a stowaway. It is race-hatred. Punishment for Qui and his cousin being Chinese. A manifestation of Japan's contempt for China. And Qui can do nothing to help. He has always been *xiǎo biǎo dì*, smaller, weaker than his cousin.

Mist thick with the stink of coal dust and sulphur wraps him like a shroud.

Focus, the first discipline.

He pictures the calligraphy brush made from his first hair cuttings by his father. Forming it whole in his mind, he takes up the slender bone handle and dabbles the rounded tuft in the yellow-grey of the mist. When the strands are water-fat he holds the quivering tip above a stretched sheet of *xuanzhi* paper. With a single slow sweep of his arm, he paints the arc of a *yuanxiang*—an almost-closed circle.

The pigment left by the stroke is barely visible. Finer than anything he ever mixed from the pine soot of his family's ink-sticks.

Fine enough, Qui hopes, to hide a life.

He jerks as a stream of Japanese blasts from the ship's Tannoy. When it stops, he hears the *wōkòu*, shouting. Through eyelashes, Qui watches his cousin being forced to his feet.

Biǎojiě, taller and heavier than his stocky attacker, staggers meekly ahead as the *wōkòu* punches savagely at his lower back.

Greyed by the mist, they pass the lifeboat that hid Qui for eight days. They round the bulkhead. Out of sight.

Qui rolls onto his stomach. He drags himself into the shadows along the ship's side and peers over the gunwale. Far below, black water glints with knives. Behind him is the roar of trucks and machinery, the shouts of dock workers. Ahead, nothing but the thickening mist.

Newcastle, his cousin said. A city. But how could this be a city? It is the middle of nowhere, like Adelaide where, in six months, he'd failed to establish one good export connection. His family's silks worth nothing. Qui's father knows he's a scholar, not a salesman, yet sent him on this onerous task, and when the news came of Japan bombing China, he still hadn't earned his passage home. It seemed like sheer good fortune when the letter came from Perth. His cousin, writing that his ship, *Silksworth*, would soon dock at Stenway Bay. After a long journey from Adelaide in a bumpy truck, Qui had waited for hours on the loading wharf, rehearsing the arguments to convince his cousin to hide him on the ship. When *Biǎojiě* finally appeared, covered in the powdered gypsum his ship was loading, Qui was almost as white.

'Our families, our city, our warehouses are being attacked,' Qui told his cousin, but each plea was countered with 'Too dangerous.' On the verge of giving up, he'd said, '*Biǎojiě*, when you came down that gangplank, but for your height and your familiar walk, I would not have known you. You look like a ghost. Now I look the same. Another ghost on your ship. Who will know?'

What a fool. Endless days jammed in a lifeboat between oars and ropes, unable to lift the canvas for fresh air in daylight. Seeing *Biǎojiě* only in the dark, when he passed in food and water and took the waste, with his constant warnings to keep out of sight of the Japanese officers. Last night, when *Biǎojiě* hastily whispered, 'A *wōkòu* has bashed one of our seamen. Don't lift this cover even for air', Qui had quietly laughed at the old-fashioned insult. '*Wōkòu*? You call your officers pirates?' His cousin had hissed 'Pirates, marauders, murderers. Never laugh at a dangerous man.'

Every part of Qui aches, but that is irrelevant now.

He stares down the length of the ship. Beyond the downstream dock lights, a pale glow throbs in the mist. A Lighthouse? Death's cold heart? In the end it was *Biǎojiě* who was incautious, coming in daylight with money, saying urgently that the Chinese crew were deserting ship in protest, and local dockworkers had agreed to help. 'Wait for dark,' he said. 'Find passage.'

But his words had been cut short by the enraged *wōkòu*'s shout.

Qui grasps the edge of the gunwale. It is time. He has failed one promise to his cousin, to stay invisible, he will not fail the other. For who will accept a mad *wōkòu*'s story when there is no body for proof?

He brings the perfection of the *yuanxiang* back into his mind. *Ensō*, the Japanese call the calligraphy circle. A thing of beauty they once shared with China.

He falls like an anchor. Sinking into the cold dark he sees the water above him as a swirl of dirty light. The circle, closing.

Who will have a fishy, on a little dishy?

Singing, Minnow hauls off her shoes, stows them beneath the dinghy's seat and spreads her toes in the cold air. They have blistered again from the long walk down Ingall Street—her feet might fit into her mother's long-unworn shoes, but the stiff leather is taking its time to soften.

Who will have a fishy, when the boat comes in?

Min sits for a moment, sniffing in the familiar scents of mud, weeds and fishiness, mingled with the tarry creosote on Black Wharf's splintery piers. Smells that have threaded the texture of her childhood growing up on the delta islands of the Hunter River—or *Coquun*, as Min's best friend, Kirra, calls it in her language. Kirra lives with her family on Dempsey, the island right next to Mosquito Island, where Min and her dad live, and she says her people have called the river *Coquun* forever.

Tonight, those comforting river smells are overlaid with coal smoke and the tang of hot metal from the immense BHP Steelworks downstream. Min glances behind to where the dusk-darkened sheds and machinery rear tall against the ruddy glow from fires in the steel mill. The noise from the Works is like the smoke-taste in the back of her throat, constant and oppressive. But she is warmed by the thought of shift workers, their jobs secure, trudging home to their families and stoking their stoves against the evening chill while the steel mill glows on through the night.

Her dinghy, Coracle, jerks against its painter like a springing horse. Readying the oars, Min pulls a wooden reel from beneath her seat. A dried prawn is fused to the hook. A catch is unlikely, but luck is never out of the question. The line snickers over the side. She notches it and wedges the reel within reach. Upstream, Spit Island sits like a cowpat against the fading pink sky. A full moon tonight. It must be close to rising.

She casts off and hauls hard on one oar. The tide is running in fast. She'll need to row downstream to the Steelworks before turning to cross. Coracle skims, despite the current. Named for Ben Gunn's boat in *Treasure Island*, 'the first and the worst coracle ever made by man,' the dinghy was a wreck when her dad saw it among the dumped boats in Rotten Row. They took it home on a neighbour's cart and, over months of her dad teaching her between his shifts at the Works, they replaced the rotten timbers with new, planing and bending each piece to fit. After her dad's accident at work, when his hands were burnt, Min did all the work herself. With money tight, when the gaps were finally calked and the dinghy ready for painting, she had to abandon her dream of beautiful colours and make do with an old tin of lumpy white, thinned with turps. 'White's best anyway, love,' Dad said. 'I'll spot you quicker coming across the river.' But soon after, she'd started her first job at the Ingall Street Emporium, and when her boss, Mr Marshall, asked about the paint flecks on her hands, she explained what she'd been up to and he'd offered the left-over paint from his new shopfront sign. Now Coracle sports a yolk-yellow transom and gunwales, with its name in looped black letters on the bows.

The curls against Min's cheeks feel clammy. She looks behind. A high bank of cloud has rolled in from the sea. Lit by the dock lights, it looks like dirty cottonwool. She frowns. Sea mist, a king tide, and no sign of the moon. She ships the oars, feeling her boat lose way as she thrusts her springy red hair down the neck of her coat. 'Red is a *breá* colour, my girl, and be glad it's curly,' Mam used to say. 'Besides, no amount of wishing will make it any other way.' Mam was right, Min thinks sadly. Wishing never changes anything.

Rowing hard again, she jumps at a sudden nearby rumble. The air fills with the hiss and metallic stink of hot slag meeting the water. Another rail wagon of waste from the Works being dumped along the riverbank, she thinks uneasily. Having grown up with this river, she knows it like the back of her hand, and it upsets her seeing that the inlets and shallows where the fish breed, the mangroves where the birds like to nest, and the huge shell heaps where, for centuries, Aboriginal people gathered to feast, are vanishing beneath the Works' ever-encroaching slag mounds. The river and its banks disposable. Like the Company's workers. Too many accidents happen at the Works, like the terrible burns to her dad's hands from when he pulled poor Billy Sims from a spill at the blast furnace, even though Billy was already dead.

Min forces her thoughts away from that horror, imaging instead her father's face when she tells him of the latest union win. A pay rise for shop assistants. In a month, when she turns seventeen, there'll be an extra shilling a week in her pay packet. And her dad, after all, is the reason Mr Marshall offered her work at the Emporium. Billy Sims was Mrs Marshall's nephew.

Her shoulders ache. Surely she has rowed far enough? Mist snakes around her as she swings Coracle towards Mosquito Island, keeping her balance as the dinghy pitches in the river's surge. She isn't scared. Her dad has drummed in everything she needs to know to keep safe. She scans the dark shapes of the island as the dingy picks up speed, but there are no familiar house lights beyond the mangroves, no bobbing lantern to show her dad coming to meet her in the inlet between Mosquito, and Dempsey Island. The mist overtakes her. Rowing blind, she aims for the mangroves. She will probably get horribly scratched, but the water will be calmer.

A horizontal shape looms ahead. The Heron Tree? Could she have overshot by that far? Min releases one oar and crouches, ready to brace. With a sickening thump the dinghy hits the half-submerged trunk. As it swings hard about, the oar slides from the rowlock. She lunges to catch it and, Jesusmaryandjoseph, a hand is clawing out of the river, there's a face beneath her capsizing boat.

She shrieks for her father as Coracle flips her into the shock of cold water.

Min stinks of mud and can't stop shivering. Wrapped in her father's old army coat, she sits so close to the blaze her dad has built in the fireplace that her face is almost burning. Kirra's uncle, old Alf Wellington, and his son, Boot, sit nearby on wooden boxes with their hands wrapped around enamel mugs full of tea as old Alf relives the drama.

'T'wasn't for that fog we'd still be out on the Oyster Banks. Thought you was an owl at first, girlie. Good thing you've got strong lungs.' He breaks into a hacking laugh and noisily clears his throat. 'The Heron Tree, who'd've known? I always reckoned that flood twenty year ago must've put that old tallowwood there for a purpose. Landmark by day and a proper bugger in the dark, but it caught you up.' He nods towards the shape huddled beneath hessian sacks and an old blanket on the far side of the stove. 'And you saved that lad. Little trooper, you are.'

'Minnow. Lives right up to that name, she does. Better'n a fish in water.' Boot looks intently into his mug, his face flushing.

It is the longest speech Min has heard Boot make. She wants to say, 'Call me Margaret, not Minnow.' But how can she abandon the pet-name Mam gave her? And it's not as if she knows Boot's real name, either.

The kerosene lamp casts a yellow gleam on the forehead of the man in the blankets. Black hair, smooth skin, not old like her dad. She wills him to open his tightly closed eyes, certain that he's not asleep but listening. Suddenly overwhelmed with wonder that they are both still alive, she pulls her dad's coat tighter. On the island, she has grown up with life and death. Calves and lambs dropping to the ground in a mess of bloody membrane, the disturbing mating of horses, a puppy born with its brain glistening where there should have been skull. She nursed her mother as she coughed her life away and still tends to the suppurating horror of her dad's burnt hands. She even saw little Reggie Mills' grey body brought back to Black Wharf a week after he fell into the river, his mother Maeve wailing, 'I only turned away for a moment,' as she reached wildly to the men who passed him up, Reggie's skin sloughing in the clutch of her hands. But tonight, Min's world turned hostile. Survival became personal.

The waterpot over the fire starts to steam. Boot jumps up. Using his jacket sleeve to grasp the hot handle, he carries it out to the lean-to.

Min insists that she is warm enough and will go second in the tin bath. She watches her father walk over to the shape lying inert under the coverings. He bends, and nudges with his bandaged hand where a shoulder might be.

Clutching the blanket tightly around himself, the young man climbs to his feet. His face is bloody, and he looks dazed. Head bowed, he says haltingly, 'I am Qui. Help, please. Tell no one.'

Min's dad shushes him. 'It's alright lad, we'll sort you out tomorrow. There are blokes like you on the island. Chinese gardeners. Good men. They'll look after you.'

Min, dressed in her flannel nightgown, presses her cheek against the cold glass of her bedroom window. Her damp hair has been untangled by concentrated brushing. The young man had bathed quickly, managing to clean himself well with the washcloth before he got in the bath. Having tried unsuccessfully to follow his example, she'd climbed into water that was still warm, and nearly clear.

Despite having scrubbed herself all over, she can still smell mangroves. She moves the lantern close and picks at the mud under her fingernails. His slippery fingers had latched so tight on her arm she'd had to prise them off. How cold she'd been, trying to keep his head above water as she clung to the old tree, her bare feet in the sucking mud, her voice hoarse from screaming. Then the fishermen's shouts. Their rough, rescuing hands.

The fishermen have gone with Min's dad to look for Coracle, Old Alf adamant that if it is damaged or lost he and Boot will be back with their boat in the morning to take her across the river.

No need to spell out that a day's pay can't be missed.

Outside, the mist has vanished and the high moon shines hard and insistent. The night has a dangerous glitter, everything silver-sharp, the leaves of the giant Moreton Bay fig trees, grass blades and puddles, fenceposts, stones along the track.

Min shivers. Everything she's known until now seems insignificant. She feels a strange sense of unfurling, the way a bracken shoot slowly uncurls from a tight knot and transforms into a green frond.

She listens. There is no sound in the house. He must be sleeping. Chinese, she thinks. *Qui*. She walks softly to her door and eases it open a crack.

Clad in only her dad's old serge pants, Qui sits cross-legged amongst the bedding. His body is lean and his skin, except where it looks torn or bruised, is smooth. She watches him arch his back and circle his shoulders, un-crick his neck. He reaches for the squat candle on the floor beside him. Breaking it from its hold on the saucer, he begins to inspect his wounds. His skin glows gold where the flame approaches. After he is done, he sits curve-backed and stares at the candle clutched in both of his hands.

The flicker of light on his face and chest, and the subtle shifting of his shadow on the wall, are the only movements in the room.

Min is about to return to bed, when he moves again. Bracing his left arm on his knee, he holds the candle above the soft inner skin of his forearm and tilts a thin stream of the molten wax.

Unable to bear the rawness, Min opens the door.

Qui keeps his eyes fixed on the wax circle congealing on his arm, as she kneels in front of him. No acknowledgement.

I could be a ghost, she thinks, as she takes the candle from his unresisting fingers. She tilts it over the saucer to pool more wax, and refastens it.

His skin is warm under her cold fingers. After she has peeled the wax circle from his arm, she slides her palm to the veins inside his wrist, the throb of his pulse.

He can't look at her, but he reaches to touch the damp hair that falls over her shoulder. Tendrils, lit red by the candlelight, spill from his shaking fingers.

Mrs O'Keefe, having exhausted every detail of her daughter's impending marriage at the Stockton Seaman's Mission—sewing the wedding gown, organising to collect flowers from her neighbours, each sandwich and cake she will produce for the banquet—returns to agonising over the extravagance of buying Jap-silk for sewing the wedding-night negligee.

Min stands behind the shop counter, barely listening. She is thinking of Qui's fingers, long, slender, his touch nearly as soft as a woman's. All the men she knows, even the Chinese gardeners on the island, have big-knuckled, work-calloused hands.

Mr Marshall, emerging from the back office, falters when he sees Min's customer, but retreat is impossible. With barely a pause for breath, Mrs O'Keefe calls, 'A hundred Chinamen, Mr Marshall. A hundred! Storming off that cargo ship from Adelaide. Shocking, don't you think?'

Mr Marshall advances to the edge of politeness. 'Thirty-six seamen, I believe, Mrs O'Keefe. And in protest against their brutal treatment, I understand. I consider it a terrible state of affairs, Japan starting this war with China. And fortunate that our union workers are keen to support the sailors' plight.'

'But all those Orientals, walking freely around our streets?' Fanning her flushed cheek with a plump hand, Mrs O'Keefe tilts her head toward Min. 'Think what could happen, Mr Marshall.'

'Not walking freely, Mrs O'Keefe,' Mr Marshall says mildly, 'Perhaps you also read that the Chinese sailors surrendered to the police and have been put in the cells for their own safety. They have asked for protection. All they want is a safe passage home.'

Mrs O'Keefe sighs heavily. She turns back to fingering the silks. Min's attention drifts again. Last week, she met Mr Marshall's partner in the Emporium. A handsome man in a smart suit, who Mr Marshall introduced as 'My good friend Mr Li.'

'Pay attention, girl!'

Startled, Min quickly hoists the bolt of peacock blue brocade Mrs O'Keefe is pointing to, and follows her customer's march towards the shop mirror. As she helps to drape the shiny fabric across the stout body, Min pictures the faces of the Chinese families who live on the island. Quiet, hardworking, gentle people. Unsettled by Mrs O'Keefe's reaction to the news of the Chinese seamen, she wonders, which parts of any story are real, and which are imagined?

All her life, when asked what made her decide on a career with the unions, or probed about her daughter Mai's glossy black hair and golden skin, Min will laugh and say, 'Oh, if you need the answer to that you'll have to ask the moon.'

So much to blame on the moon. Which hid, that night on the river, only to return later, full and urgent.

02: 1977 Aviary

Marty thumped up the three sets of concrete stairs to the top level of the flats. The yellow light leaking through the venetian blinds of the window at the far end of the roofless walkway told him his mum was home. Above him the clouds looked like the grey stuff that comes out of old mattresses, and the air had the rotten egg stink of the Steelworks. Sometimes it ponged at night in their old Waratah house too, but never like down here in Mayfield, overlooking the Works.

Last winter, Dad explained why Newcastle got smelly in cold weather. 'When the clouds are low and cover the sky, they trap the warm air beneath with the smog. It's called a temperature inversion. Like how the blankets trap your farts in bed.'

Marty missed his dad's jokes. He missed those rough carpenter's hands and the smell of his work clothes: sawdust mixed with sweat and Brut deodorant. Once he'd asked, 'Why's it called Brut?' and Dad had laughed, 'No mate, you can't say it like that. You have to say 'Broote,' like a Frenchie.' Taking a deep sniff of his hairy armpit, he said, 'Stops brutes like me being stinky.'

Marty missed their house in Harriet Street, too. Sitting on the landing of the back concrete stairs while Dad had a beer in the evening. You could see right over where they were building the new shopping village for Waratah. Dad worked there as a chippie, and he'd point out what was happening with the cranes and tell funny stories about the other workers. Marty remembers when the Waratah Brickworks were demolished to make way for the shops. The Brickworks' chimney reached right up to the clouds. Dad promised to go down to Coolamin Road to watch it come down, but Mum said that was too dangerous, so they watched from the landing. When it hit the ground, a massive cloud of black dust spurted into the sky and their house wobbled.

Spike's cage still hung from its hook at the end of the walkway. There was a black shape below it on the balustrade. 'Piss off shit-cat,' Marty shouted, breaking into a run. The cat scuttled past. Marty's mum hated him using swear words, but he could hear the TV on full blast.

Spike was huddled against the mirror on the top perch. As Marty lifted the cage down, the yellow and green feathers of the bird's flapping wings caught strips of light. Marty whispered through the bars, 'I'm just another scary shape out here, aren't I little fella? She should have brought you inside.'

Marty slammed the door as he walked in and felt bad when Spike fluttered in fright to the cage floor. Mum was on the couch, watching Pot of Gold. She gave a backwards wave when Marty said a gruff hello. He hung the cage on its stand in the laundry, undid the twist of wire that kept the cage door shut. Inserting his hand slowly, he nudged the budgie until it climbed onto his finger, and brought the little bird carefully out. Marty held Spike to his face to warm him with his breath, tutting and nuzzling until his trembling subsided.

With Spike perched on his shoulder, Marty looked for the budgie seed, which he found beside the tea canister in the kitchen.

'You didn't bring Spike in before dark,' he shouted. When his mum didn't react, he crossed the room to block her view of the TV.

'The cat from the place next door was outside.'

She shuffled sideways on the couch to peer around him.

'Right beneath Spike. Up on the parapet.'

'Sorry.' Her eyes stayed fixed on the screen.

Marty filled Spike's bird feeder, fished a drowned green feather from the water container, and topped it up. He returned the budgie to his perch, re-twisted the door wire and wrapped his cage in an old Indian shawl.

'Night little fella.'

In his bedroom, Marty levered off his Dunlop Volleys, wet from kicking the soccer ball around with Damo in the long grass of Tourle Street Reserve. The first time he wore them to school, Damo stamped dirt and grass all over them, saying, 'Get rid of the white, dickhead, else you're gunna look like a girl.'

Marty sniffed with satisfaction. These days, the Volleys stank even worse than the smog. He flung them beside the wardrobe, stripped off his clothes, grabbed his towel and ran to the bathroom. Counting under his breath, he soaped himself furiously under the stream of hot water, giving his willy a tug before he rinsed off. But what Damo reckoned would happen still didn't. At the exact count of 120, he turned the taps off. Two minutes was plenty for a bloke-shower, Dad always said.

Marty pushed back the shower curtain and dried himself roughly with his towel. Using one corner, he wiped the fog off the vanity mirror, revealing blue eyes and shoulder-length blond hair. He grabbed a comb and tried to drag his curls straight. It never worked. He leant close and rubbed at a red blotch on his upper lip, in case it was a bristle trying to get through, but there was no moustache-progress. Dimitri in Grade 6B at school, who reckons he'd already shaved twice, called Marty a baby-face with no hope in hell, because no one would ever want to see a girly blond moustache. Angling his face to the mirror, Marty checked the side of his cheek. He desperately wanted sideburns. Not reddish like his dad's were, although that felt a bit disloyal. Marty wanted dark sideburns. Like Father Frank's.

'Frank by name and frank by nature.'

That's what Father Frank told Marty's mum, the first time he called around for a visit. It was a Thursday and Marty had just arrived home from school. Sitting at the messy kitchen table, Father Frank said, 'Please, absolutely no need to call me Father, except at Church.' He smiled at Marty. 'You too, son. You can call me Frank if you like.'

Marty liked being called 'son' but decided to stick with the 'Father,' even though his mum didn't.

After Father Frank left, he asked, 'What does frank by nature mean?'

His mum thought for a bit.

'I suppose it means Father Frank will always say what he thinks. That's the type of man he is.'

Frank by name and frank by nature sounded like how old men talk. But Father Frank didn't look much older than Marty's mum, and she was way younger than Damo's mum. The priest's face was always tanned and his sideburns and eyebrows were brown, even though his hair on the top was blond. If it had been a bit longer, he could have passed for a surfie.

'Don't you think Father Frank looks a bit like Harrison Ford, Marty?'

Marty and his mum were walking out of the Lyrique Theatre, after seeing Star Wars.

'Who's Harrison Ford?'

Mum laughed, 'Oh, you know, Han Solo.'

'I guess so.'

But Marty didn't really get it. Sure, Father Frank was tall like Han. He even had the same roughish skin on his face and sort of unavoidable brown eyes. But Father Frank parted his hair on one side in a straight line and made it sit flat with Brylcreem like the other priests. Father Frank didn't look like he'd win a fight, either. But he was a hero in a different way. Because of Spike.

Marty's twelfth birthday was his first without his dad. Mum cried when she handed him his present at breakfast. He ripped open the rocket ship paper. Inside was a Sony transistor, a bit scratched but it worked fine. There was a card with $10 inside and his mum had written 'With love from Mum and Dad'. Sticky-taped beneath was a paper strip in Dad's handwriting. Which said, 'I love you matey, sorry I'm not there for your birthday.' Marty cried too.

At school, Marty's class sang Happy Birthday and Mrs Rubbo brought her usual big marble cake with chocolate icing.

Home again, Marty was mucking around with the transistor in his room, when he heard a knock. His mum called from the couch, 'Marty, can you get it?'

Marty opened the door to Father Frank holding a wire cage. Inside it was a scared-looking gold and green budgie. Father Frank put the cage on the kitchen table and Marty's mum made a pot of tea.

Father Frank pulled a paper bag full of seed from his pocket. 'You'll need to check your bird's seed and water each day, and put fresh newspaper in its tray on Saturdays. Give it a few days to settle before you try to get it out of the cage. When you think it's ready, put your hand slowly inside and hold your finger under its chest, like this.'

Father Frank held his forefinger sideways. With a sudden laugh, he poked Marty in the ribs. 'Gotcha.'

Marty giggled. He opened the cage and moved his hand carefully inside.

'That's it. Remember, slow and quiet until it gets used to you. It'd be a good idea to do this in the kitchen with the door closed, in case it takes fright and you have to catch it.'

The little bird jumped on Marty's finger. He could hardly believe the tight clutch of claws, their miniscule warmth.

Marty's mum, pouring the tea, asked, 'Is it a boy or a girl?'

'It's a lovely little boy,' Father Frank told her. 'And quite young. It came from Albie, a good friend of mine. Albie says if you handle a bird young, it won't be afraid and you can get it to do what you want. You can train it to come to you, and teach it to talk.'

'What sort of talk?' Marty let the little bird hop back on its perch, still not quite believing it was his.

'Oh, things like Hello, or Pretty Boy.'

'Try teaching him this, Marty.'

His mum leaned close to the cage and said in a giggly voice, 'Where's Father Frank? Where's Father Frank?'

Marty laughed. 'I'll get him to say that every time someone knocks at the door.'

He wished his voice hadn't sounded squeaky, like his mum's.

That year, Marty's birthday fell on the Tuesday in June following the Queen's Birthday holiday. He liked the Queen. It was her visit to Newcastle a while back, in March, that helped his mum to stop being so sad. The day Mum and Father Frank started to become friends.

Father Frank had mentioned after Mass that he planned to go to Civic Park to see the Queen and Prince Phillip. After church, Mum had told Father Frank that she thought she and Marty might go too. Mum had her hair cut so it was bouncy, and on the Queen day she wore a dress Dad used to really like. There were little white buttons all the way down the front and the pink material had swirly shapes all over it. Marty remembered his dad saying the pattern was called paisley, and if Marty thought of parsley, he would always remember the right word.

Mum found a spot right beside the marked-off walkway in Civic Park. So, they saw the Queen up close. She didn't stop to talk, but the

Newcastle Herald had a photo with Marty and Mum in it. Mum was smiling and looked really nice. Marty was looking the wrong way so all you could see were stupid curls. After the Queen had gone, Mum waved at Father Frank who was standing with some other priests. He came over to say hello. Mum's face went red when he said, 'That dress is even prettier than Her Majesty's.'

They had a lot to say. Marty kicked at the side of the concrete path until he heard someone shout 'Hey, Mart-Fart.' He saw Damo. up beside the fountain, throwing sticks into the water. Marty charged up the steps to give him a hand.

Mum and Father Frank kept talking on and on. A couple of times Father Frank looked up towards Marty and waved.

After that, Marty's mum started going to church during the week. She said Father Frank was helping her sort out her thinking. He began to visit more often, on Thursdays, after Marty arrived home from school. Marty's mum fussed more about the flat now, cleaning up, making it look nice. She went to Vinnies and bought a Madonna for the corner table in the living room. Two of Our Lady's fingers were missing, but you couldn't really tell. She brought out the picture of Jesus that she'd had in her bedroom since she was a kid, and Marty helped her hammer a nail in the wall beside the TV. Jesus looked up to heaven with big shiny blue eyes. The old frame was shabby, so Mum draped a filmy red scarf over the sides of the frame. Jesus looked weird, like there was extra blood coming from his crown of thorns.

Marty pulled on his pyjamas, thinking how things had been a lot better since Spike appeared. After Father Frank left, Marty heard his mum humming while she wiped the kitchen table. He recognised the tune but couldn't remember the name, so he asked her. She didn't answer. He asked again and she said, 'Sorry Marty, I was miles away,' and scrunched her fingers in his hair. She hadn't done that for a while. Which was basically a good thing, because scrunching made it curl even more. 'How nice of Father Frank. A lovely surprise,' Mum said, and she tutted at the budgie through the wires of the cage. 'How pretty he is, Marty, like a little daffodil. We'll have to think of a name.'

'I'm calling him Spike.'

'Spike? But he's so smooth and neat.'

'It's Spike.'

Mum had started to giggle. She slumped to the table with her head on her arms and laughed. Marty didn't know what was funny, but joined in anyway. He hadn't heard her laugh in ages.

There had been other changes too. His mum hardly ever used to listen to the radio, but now she phoned 2KO with requests. And she watched Countdown with him. One night The Ferrets were singing *Don't Fall in Love* and Marty remembered it was the song she hummed the day Father Frank brought Spike. He told Mum. She just said The Ferrets' singer was cute, but it was a stupid name for a band. Marty always wanted a ferret. Back in Harriet Street, Dad had promised to get him one for a pet, but Mum said they were horrible animals that bit and stank.

Marty put on his slippers and went to the kitchen to make dinner. Taking a bag of squashed sliced bread from the fridge's small freezer, he yelled to his mum, 'Baked beans or soup?'

She yelled back over the shrieking Pot of Gold audience, 'You choose.'

Marty opened a tin of Cream of Chicken soup and while it heated, prised six slices of bread apart to put in the toaster.

Carrying his mum's plate to her, he realised she never complained about Spike's poo. She just said, 'Leave it to dry and pick it up later.' But she wouldn't notice the budgie poo stink, because she didn't clean out the cage.

Marty wondered uneasily how long budgies lived. He cheered up at the thought that the next day was Thursday. Father Frank would know.

'Sorry son, I have no idea.'

Marty felt deflated. But Father Frank was saying to Marty's mum, 'I'm planning to visit my friend Albie on Saturday. He lives out Cessnock way. He's sure to know the answer because he's bred birds for years. He's known Spike right from when he was a tiny egg in the nest. I tell you what! Why don't you both come too? A drive in the country.'

Marty's mum clapped her hands. 'A picnic? I could make sandwiches. Bring a thermos of tea.'

Father Frank leaned back in the rocker chair, something else Marty's mum had got from Vinnies op shop. She worked there as a volunteer now, two days a week during school hours. That had been Father Frank's idea, and the Vinnies supervisor, Ted, told Mum she could have the rocker for free. He even brought it home in the Vinnies truck and Marty helped carry it up the stairs. Ted was big, with grey curly hair, a growly voice and a red nose. His whole face was red by the time they got the chair up three flights. He used words Marty had never heard before and dropped his g's and h's, which Mum was always telling Marty not to do. After Ted left, she said he came from somewhere in England where people spoke like that.

'Sandwiches, now that would be grand,' Father Frank was saying. 'And perhaps some cake? Don't worry about the thermos though. Albie is sure to offer us a cuppa.'

Marty loved the drive out to Aberdare, with Father Frank telling them about the towns they went through, and the names of the big hills. At one stage his mum said, 'Shush, Marty, too many questions.' When Father Frank turned the car off the gravel road and into a driveway that went through scrubby trees, she said, 'Why would your friend want to live way out here in the bush?' Father Frank chuckled, 'Oh, Albie loves it out here. He likes a quiet life, and it's perfect for his birds.'

'You'll get about ten years out of your budgie, if you treat him right,' Albie told Marty. He looked older than Father Frank, a little man with a round face, who reminded Marty of the drawings of Friar Tuck in his Robin Hood book. They were standing outside the budgie cages. *Aviaries*, Albie called them. The cages had welded gates with big padlocks, bird-wire over the top and sides, and corrugated iron at the back. For extra shelter, Albie said. Inside there were dry branches and straight bits of wood propped up for perches, with boxes with small round holes at the front wired to them. Seeds and feathers and grey and white bird poo splotched the concrete floor. It smelled musty, like Spike-poo, only stronger. There were budgies of all colours, blue, green, yellow, a purpley colour, even white ones. Marty watched them flit from branch to perch and wondered if Spike would rather be back with his mates instead of in his small cage with occasional flutters around their flat. He plucked up the courage to ask Albie why the green budgies were separate. 'So that we don't get too many of that colour,' Albie said. 'If you want a special colour like purple and blue you have a better chance if the parents have that colour. Green is too ordinary.'

Marty couldn't help feeling glad that Spike was mostly yellow.

The budgie cages looked way nicer than the cocky cage, where there were some big white cockatoos, and two black ones with red under their tails, and some plainer ones with pink and grey feathers. The smaller birds flew around when Albie banged the wire of the cage but there wasn't enough room for the big cockies to do much except flap. One old looking cocky, with scabby legs and dirty white feathers, flapped awkwardly to the concrete. It picked up a stick with its curved beak, held it with one claw and split it open. The wood fell to the floor and the cocky pecked it into small pieces.

Marty pointed. 'Why is he doing that?'

Albie laughed. 'In the wild, cockatoos pull grubs out of trunks and branches. They can do a lot of damage to a tree. That old feller thinks he's going to get lucky, but he never is.'

Marty felt sorry for the cocky. He remembered the story of Abraham and his son in the picture Bible, and the word *sacrifice* floated into his head. He watched the cocky stomp back to its tree, really just an old leafless branch stuck in the ground. It used its beak to help climb awkwardly back to the top, where it sat looking hunched and sad. Suddenly it spread its wings, raised its yellow crest, and let out an enormous shriek.

Marty's mum jumped. 'Goodness, what an awful noise.'

Marty was hungry. He kicked at a rusty steel bar half buried in the ground. Why did adults have to talk so much? Father Frank and Albie kept laughing about things that happened when they were priests together in some other place.

'Stop doing that, Marty, no wonder your shoes wear out so fast,'

Marty's mum said crossly.

Father Frank and Albie looked at her. She smiled, and said in a changed voice, 'He is always kicking things. Even in church. I have to stop him from kicking the pews. Look at the state of his shoes. They cost a fortune.'

Father Frank said, 'I'm starving, aren't you Marty? It must be time for our picnic. I'm certainly looking forward to those sandwiches.'

Marty's mum had worried about what sort of sandwiches to make, but in the end she settled on Pecks Fish Paste, and Empire sausage because it looked nicer than Devon. And she bought a Franklins' square fruit cake, like at Christmas.

They left soon after lunch because Father Frank had things to do before Mass the next day. Marty's mum had talked a lot on the way out to Albie's place, but now she was quiet. She asked Father Frank if he could turn on the radio. A hymn came on. Marty knew his mum liked 2KO better than 2NX, the Catholic station, but she didn't say anything. He had a feeling that she didn't like Albie very much.

After Father Frank dropped them back at the flats, Marty's mum said, 'What a strange little man that Albie was. And his house. Don't you think it was weird, Marty, all that old dark furniture and fancy ornaments? Not the sort of house you'd expect a man to live in really, especially out in the bush. Did you notice not one thing was out of place? I felt so uncomfortable, sitting at that polished wood table in case I slopped my tea or dropped crumbs. And I am sure he hated the sandwiches.'

'Father Frank dropped plenty of crumbs. I did too. And the chocolate mint biscuits were yum.' Marty's mouth filled with saliva at the thought.

His mum grumbled, 'Well, I thought that as Albie didn't even open our cake, he could have suggested we bring it back home.'

Marty didn't mind Albie, but he did look a bit funny with his little feet and curved-out legs and round stomach. He seemed to know everything about birds though. Marty liked the budgies best, and the small grey parrots with butter-yellow heads and crests and round pink patches on their cheeks, were pretty. Albie told him they were cockatiels, and they made good pets.

Marty wanted to see more of the birds and learn all the different names. Maybe he would ask Father Frank if he and his mum could go out there again sometime.

Marty didn't have to ask. The following Thursday Father Frank arrived with something wrapped in brown paper. He said, 'Well, son, did you enjoy our little excursion out to Albie's?

Marty nodded vigorously.

'I hope these do the trick.' Father Frank handed the parcel to Marty's mum.

Marty's mum seemed to guess what was inside. As she undid the string, she said, 'For Marty? Because of my outburst at Albie's place?'

The brown leather shoes gleamed with polish.

'Oh Frank, you *are* thoughtful. I shouldn't have complained. I'll make the tea, and Marty, take Father Frank into the lounge room to see if they fit.'

No kid at school wears shoes like this, Marty thought. Only the old men teachers. He unlaced one hoping desperately it would be the wrong size. His foot slid in easily. Bumps and hollows told him someone else had worn them. He wouldn't have minded if they had been Father Frank's shoes, but Father Frank's feet were big. Marty remembered Albie's feet. Small, like his hands. Father Frank didn't have a parcel when they left Albie's place last Saturday. Had he gone back out to Aberdare to get them? The thought of his feet being in Albie's shoes made Marty feel creeped out.

Marty's mum put the tea tray on the low table, and knelt to check the space at the end of his toes.

'Do they feel good, Marty? They look perfect to me.'

Father Frank stirred sugar into his tea, saying, 'I spoke to Albie on the phone this morning. He thanked you for the sandwiches and said it was a pleasure to meet a lad so interested in birds. If you'd like to visit again, I can let you know when I'm going next.'

'What a lovely offer, Frank, please do. Marty hasn't stopped talking about the place. He'd love to go back, wouldn't you, Marty?'

It took three weeks before Father Frank mentioned going back to

Aberdare. By then Marty's mum had landed a paid job on Saturdays at the St Vinnies store.

'I can't believe my luck, Marty. I'd only been a volunteer for a few weeks. Ted finds it hard to get someone to work on the weekend and Father Frank said there was money in the church coffers, so why not employ someone to keep the shop open. It's not much pay, really, but every bit counts.'

When Father Frank invited them both back to Aberdare, Marty's mum said, 'Oh, what a pity I'll be working. But I don't see why Marty can't go. You won't mind me not coming, will you Marty? It will be more fun than a day hanging around here alone.'

Marty was super excited to go to Aberdare without his mum. That visit, he worked out that Albie didn't breed birds just because he loved them. It was a business. Father Frank asked if any birds had sold during the week, and Albie said a buyer was coming that evening to pick up six pairs of cockatiels.

'You've come at a good time, young man. I already have the birds picked out. Come and have a look.'

Behind the cocky aviary was a shed Marty hadn't noticed before. It had small glass windows in the corrugated iron walls. As Albie unlocked the padlock, the birds inside began to shriek. He flicked a light switch as he walked in. A grid of cages covered the back wall. Several contained pairs of cockatiels. They flapped in agitation at the sudden light.

Albie unlatched one of the cages. 'These are all young birds, Marty. We have to get them used to handling, and these have all been handled a lot.'

He reached in, grabbed a cockatiel and held the protesting bird with his small, pale hands. 'This one still has a touch of the wild in him.'

The cockatiel calmed. Albie tickled the back of its neck with a thumb. The bird seemed to like it and bent its head forward. Marty loved how its crest feathers curved up and the round pink patch on each cheek reminded him of how he drew cheeks on faces when he was a little kid.

'Pretty boy, pretty boy,' Albie played his fingers down the length of the bird. The cockatiel, ducking away from the pressure, screeched and bit Albie's thumb.

'Jesus bloody Christ!'

Marty's fascination turned to shock. His laugh sounded like the cockatiel's squeal.

Albie thrust the bird back in the cage and sucked the blood from his thumb. With a wink at Father Frank, he said, 'It's okay Marty, we like birds with spirit.'

Suddenly he pulled Marty into a hug, so his face was pressed into Albie's spongy stomach, and he tickled Marty's neck with his fingers as if Marty was the bird. 'But we don't hurt them, really, nothing they can't handle,' Albie said, before letting go.

Confused, Marty turned away to look at the cages. The cockatiel that bit Albie was back with its mate. They huddled together on the perch, looking scared. Marty heard Father Frank say, 'Priest of the true sanctuary,' and Albie chuckled, 'The fulfilment of his plan.' When Marty turned back both men were smiling broadly.

Marty smiled back, but it had felt so weird, hearing a priest take the Saviour's name in vain. And hearing words from the Liturgy, when it wasn't Sunday.

It was late afternoon when Father Frank dropped Marty home. Marty looked up to see Spike's cage hanging on its verandah hook, where Mum must have put him after work. The sinking sun shone through the cage. There was no sign of Spike. Marty thundered up the stairs and along the walkway.

The cage door hung open, the wire clasp on the concrete below. He banged frantically on the door.

'Mum! Where's Spike? Spike's gone!'

He lurched to the parapet, whistling his signal for Spike to come. His mum joined him, calling 'Spikey! Spiiike.' Marty started to shout as well.

'Listen, Marty.' His mum sounded breathless. 'Isn't that him?'

Marty stood still. Over his pounding heart he heard a high-pitched trill.

'Where is he?'

Spike chirruped again. Marty's mum pointed towards the next-door garden. 'Is that him? In that jacaranda tree?'

Spike was a spot of sunlight amongst the tree's purple flowers. Marty screamed his name. The budgie fluttered to a higher branch.

'Keep whistling to him, Marty, same as you do inside. He always comes to you.'

'It's too far,' Marty wailed.

A sudden flash of yellow-green. Spike, flying erratically towards them. Marty's mum grabbed his jumper as he stretched over the parapet, hand out, finger horizontal. Spike's wings failed him. Half-falling, half-fluttering he turned back to the trees in the garden next door and disappeared over the metal fence.

'No, Spikey! That's where the cat lives!'

Marty was already running. He took the stairs two at a time, pelted along the footpath and scrambled over the neighbour's brick front fence.

Spike was a tiny patch of yellow among clumps of pine bark and fallen purple flowers, his chest heaving. Marty approached carefully, scooped up the unresisting bird and tucked him down the front of his school jumper.

Back in the flat, Spike clung to Marty's finger, his feathers puffed up, his grey inner eyelids closing. Marty held the bird to his mouth to warm him. 'He's still shaking, Mum.' Marty was also trembling, but he was too relieved to be angry with his mum.

'Poor little fella,' she said. 'Caged birds must find the real world quite terrifying.'

Marty's mum never used to drink alcohol. One birthday Marty's dad gave her a bottle of Cold Duck wrapped in red cellophane, but she said, 'Wine? I'm not sure I want it.'

'It's a celebration, love. To have with lunch. At least have a taste.'

Dad was cooking a roast chook and potatoes and cauliflower cheese for her especially. Dad had said he was going to get a rooster from his friend at the wire rope factory and Marty had hoped it would be the sort of rooster with big tail feathers. But Dad came home and handed Marty a bundle wrapped in greaseproof, saying 'Feel the weight of that.' The bundle was warm in Marty's hands and smelled like wet wool. The smell improved when it was cooking.

Marty and his mum sat down at the kitchen table and his dad got the Cold Duck out of the fridge. 'Here we go, nice and cold, happy birthday!' He filled two glasses, and an eggcup for Marty.

Marty's mum tried it and pulled a face. Marty did the same.

'Oh well, all the more for me then.' Dad drank his glass quickly and poured another.

After lunch Marty told his dad the chicken tasted great.

His mum said, 'It's a pity you couldn't get a hen. Roosters are always tough.'

Marty forgot about the Cold Duck until his mum asked Father Frank, on one of his visits, if he liked to drink beer. Father Frank said, 'Not beer, but perhaps an occasional brandy and dry.' Marty's mum bought a bottle called Chateau Tanunda and some dry ginger ale. She brought home other things too, now that she was working at Vinnies. Nice plates, a nearly new toaster and women's magazines. Stacks of them, in the living room and on her bedside table.

And Ted.

Sometimes Ted came with Father Frank on Thursday afternoons. They sat around with his mum, laughing and drinking their brandy and drys. Marty wasn't keen on Ted. The first time he was there, Marty arrived home from school, opened the door and smelled Brut. For a giddy second, he thought that his dad had come home.

'You remember Ted, don't you Marty?' his mum said.

Ted wore a blue checked shirt and a cardigan and shorts even though it was still cold. He shook Marty's hand hard enough to hurt. When Marty asked if he was wearing Brut, his mum said, 'Marty, don't be so rude,' but Ted laughed. 'Thee're a weird'un sonny. 'Appen it is Brut but 'int deodorant, it's *cologne*.'

The Thursday afternoons that Ted appeared, Marty only hung around for a bit to chat with Father Frank, before going to listen to his transistor in his bedroom. He and Damo had started making a list of all the songs on the radio they thought were ace.

The next time Marty went to Aberdare, he and Father Frank helped Albie build a new cage for some ring-necks Albie was planning to breed. Afterwards, they went into the budgie cage and Albie hoisted Marty up so he could see into two of the nesting boxes. The first female refused to move, but a blue budgie flew out of the second box leaving two pale little eggs nestled among bits of straw and feathers. The best part of the day came later, when Albie brought out a book to show Marty what ring-necks looked like. Pretty blue and green parrots with a yellow collar. Sitting at the polished table beside Albie, Marty learned lots about other birds in the book too.

When it was time to leave, Albie gave Marty the book as a present.

On the drive home Father Frank said, 'This trip gets a bit long, doesn't it? You know, I sometimes stay out there on a Friday night, at Albie's place and you could too, if you like. What do you think? Should we ask your mum?'

Back at the flats, Father Frank went upstairs with Marty. His mum looked doubtful.

'A camp out? You mean in a tent?'

'Oh, he won't be in a tent,' Father Frank reassured her. 'Albie has a bunkhouse, quite well set up.'

'A bunkhouse? Marty, would you like that? It would make weekends less boring for you, wouldn't it?'

She looked back at Father Frank. 'That's a big step for Marty though. You don't think he's too young to stay in a bunkhouse alone?'

'I'm *twelve*, mum!' Marty couldn't believe she would ask that.

Father Frank winked at Marty. 'Tell you what. Perhaps Marty has a school friend he'd like to invite along? That would be more fun than being with two oldies like Albie and me.'

'Oh, Frank, how can you say that? You are nowhere near as old as Albie.'

Marty liked his mum's playful voice. He grinned at Father Frank and said excitedly, 'Damo could come with me. He really likes the bush.'

'Damo, Marty? His mum said. 'Father Frank might like you to take a quieter friend.'

Father Frank chuckled, and said, 'Oh, Damo isn't a bad lad. A little rough around the edges, perhaps, but nothing Albie and I can't handle. I'll tuck him under my wing.'

When Marty and Damo arrived with Father Frank, Albie took them right around his place to show the fences they were not allowed to go outside. They had spaghetti and meatballs for tea, and played a really long game of Monopoly which Damo won. Then Albie and Father Frank took them out to the bunkhouse. The room Damo and Marty were in had double bunks along each side, so they each got to sleep in a top one. They had a farting competition, and told stupid stories and giggled. Then Marty felt a hand shake his shoulder, and Damo was saying, 'Wake up, ya dubbo. Coming exploring?'

It was barely daylight. They climbed through the wire fence behind Albie's big shed. Walking through the scrubby bush, they came across an old track that looked like nobody had driven on for ages. Kookaburras and magpies started calling. Soon all sorts of birds were flying from tree to tree. Marty saw finches and mudlarks and a yellow-cheeked honeyeater. They followed the track until they reached a big dam with lots of bulrushes around the edge. On the far side stood a massive round chimney, like the one that he and his dad watched fall in Waratah. Behind it was an enormous brick building with big empty arched windows and hardly any roof. Inside were big old concrete platforms with rusty machines on top and weeds and straggly bushes growing through cracks in the floor. There was lots of smashed glass from the windows and beer bottles, and rusting beer cans and other junk. It was totally grouse. On the way back to Albie's, Damo raved about how the lake would be great for swimming in summer.

It was still early when they snuck back to the bunkhouse, but Father Frank and Albie were already there, and pretty cranky. Father Frank said, after making them tell where they'd been, 'The old colliery? I'm sorry lads, we told you not to leave the property, and you are absolutely forbidden to go there. This is an old coal mining area. It is riddled with shafts and tunnels and places where young boys like you could easily have an accident.'

Albie said, 'We told you not to leave the property and there is a good reason for that. The old miners still talk about the Piewais. You'd be sorry if you met up with one of them.'

The look on his face made Marty feel a bit scared.

Damo grinned. 'Oh, yeah? What are they, the local bogeymen?'

Albie stared hard at Damo.

'You can ask anyone around here about them, laddie. Men have disappeared. You'd do well to believe me. Half-man, half-bird, they live in those tunnels around that old colliery building, and they are always hungry. The old miners say they've eaten children.'

Piewais, Marty thought. The word sounded funny. Like one Ted might use.

Afterwards Damo said that Albie was just a stupid old fart, and next time they came they should see if they could find any tunnels.

Marty, watching the hills out the car window hoped that Father Frank wouldn't say anything to his mum about him and Damo taking off.

Father Frank said, 'What's that you're singing, son?'

Marty hadn't even noticed Damo was singing in the back seat.

Damo shouted, 'It's called *The Newcastle Song*. It's on the radio and a Newcastle bloke wrote it.'

'A song about Newcastle?' Father Frank laughed. 'Sing that chorus bit again?'

Marty joined in as Damo belted out, 'Don't you ever let a chance go by, oh Lord, don't you ever let a chance go by.'

Father Frank chuckled. 'Is that a hymn? I haven't heard it before.'

Excited, Marty said, 'Oh it isn't a hymn, it's a funny pop song and the singer mostly talks, like a story with music.'

'What's the story then?'

'Um, it's about guys in cars looking at girls. And there's a bikie.'

Damo interrupted, 'Yeah, a really big bikie. The little guy, Normie, starts chatting up the bikie's girlfriend, so the bikie's gunna bash him.'

The priest laughed. 'Like David and Goliath? Does the little guy win?'

'Yeah, he does,' Damo shouted. 'The little guy's got the sense to drive away!'

Father Frank laughed even harder.

Marty was in the front seat beside Father Frank and Damo was in the back. It was Friday afternoon and they were heading out for their second camp-out at Aberdare. Marty leant his head against the car window, watching the hills rise up to Mount Vincent and Sugarloaf. He remembered the names now. He was worried about Spike. Father Frank was already at the flat when Marty got home from school so there was a rush to get his bag packed. Mum helped, then shooed them both out the door, saying 'I'll bring Spike in Marty, don't keep Father Frank waiting.' But she'd forgotten before. Mum had her nice dress on, and she went red when Father Frank said 'You look very pretty, is Ted picking you up?' She hadn't told Marty she was going out somewhere.

Albie met them at the front door.

'Take your gear out to the bunkhouse, boys. It's not so cold tonight, so we might just try out that fire-pit you helped make.'

Building the fire pit was what got Damo and Marty back in the good books, after they'd been caught out exploring the old mine. Albie told them it was their punishment, but it had been heaps of fun. They'd wheelbarrowed old rocks from along the back fence to a spot beside the bunkhouse. Some were so humungous, they had to be carried one at a time. They built a circle with the big rocks dug in upright to hold up a heavy sheet of metal they carried from the shed for the cooktop. Father Frank chainsawed a fallen-over tree into eight big rounds and Damo and Marty had races rolling them back through the garden for seats. But when they finished, and asked Albie if they could try the fireplace out, he said, no. Because of their little adventure that morning, they'd have to wait until their next visit.

This time, Marty and Damo got to build the fire. They stacked sticks into a tepee the way Marty's dad had taught him, and it caught alight first go. It was huge by the time Father Frank came out with a folding table, two bottles, and some plastic cups. Albie, following with a tray of food, said, 'Those flames are way too hot for these snags. We'll have to let them burn down.'

Sitting on a tree-round, Marty finished his fourth sausage rolled in bread. He licked a tomato sauce dribble from his hand, and decided that snags tasted even better than the smell of them cooking. Damo poked the metal plate backwards off the fire with a long stick and heaved on two big lumps of wood. Marty, Father Frank and Albie cheered as the fire sparked and blazed. Damo shouted over the crackle, 'Hey, Frank, can we try what you're drinking?'

Marty was shocked that Damo dropped the 'Father,' but Father Frank and Albie, their faces shining red in the flickery light, both laughed.

Albie said, after a glance at Father Frank, 'This is port, young man, and I'm not sure you'll like it. But finish up your Passiona and I'll give you a little taste.'

Damo drained his cup and Albie poured some wine in the bottom. Damo gulped it down, smacked his lips and grinned as he held the cup out again.

'Steady on son,' Father Frank laughed. 'This is a civilised beverage, and it needs to be drunk in a civilised way. Savoured slowly.'

With a chuckle, Albie filled the cup half full. Damo swung around. 'C'mon, Marty, don't be a retard.'

Marty thought of his mum's birthday Cold Duck as he reluctantly took over his cup. The others laughed at the face he pulled.

Father Frank picked up the Passiona bottle. 'No good, son? I'll put some of this in it to make the taste sweeter. Sit down here, near me.'

Marty watched Father Frank top up his cup and hand it back. He sipped cautiously.

'Better?'

'Much better, thank you.'

The night was really dark with hardly any stars. Beyond the fence the bush was full of sounds. Thumps and creaking, moans that sounded almost human. Damo went Oooo-ooo, oooo-ooo, and Marty shivered. Father Frank laughed. He leant to ruffle Marty's hair, which made Marty wish that his mum was there too.

Albie went back to the house and returned with a mug in each hand.

'No more wine for you boys. Hot cocoa. Drink it down and then it will be time for bed.'

That was the night the Piewais came.

Marty felt an arm slide under his shoulders. He dreamily waited for another to slide under his knees and his dad to lift him and carry him to bed. But that hadn't happened in a long time, and he was already in bed. His eyes wouldn't open. He mumbled, 'Damo?'

Hands grabbed his ankles. Marty jerked awake with a shout. '*Damo*?'

It felt like the sheet was wrapped around his head, and it was hard to breathe. He felt himself being dragged off the mattress and lifted roughly down. He started to call Damo again, but something awful and smelly was clamped hard over his nose and mouth.

Marty woke groggily. Something was tugging his willy. It became hot and wet. Vaguely, he wondered where his pyjama pants were.

When he woke again, he was lying face down. Heaviness pressed all the way along him, and there was pain. He began to cry, salt and snot seeping into his mouth. He tried to wake up properly but it was way too hard. Close to his ear, a voice said softly, 'Pretty-pretty boy.'

Marty was being lifted by his feet and his shoulders. Someone made a grunting sound. A voice near his head growled, 'Higher.'

Back on the softness of his bed, Marty's tongue felt thick and his mouth sore. He cried out, 'Damo?' but a voice snarled, 'Shuddup sonny-boy, don't you move,' and the blankets were jerked over his head. Lying rigid on his back, he heard the bunkroom door creak open. The voice muttered, 'Need a hand?' and someone else said softly, 'Nearly there.' Marty listened to footsteps which stopped at the other bunk, more grunts, noises of leaving, and the door squeal shut.

The men's voices faded, but into the silence came the distant sound of whistling. It was a tune Marty knew.

Don't you ever let a chance go by, oh Lord.

Marty dragged the blankets off his face, gagging at the lingering smell of Brut. Everywhere hurt. He rolled on to his side, pulled his knees to his chest and wrapped his arms tight around them, trying to stop trembling. But there was no way to stop the familiar voice saying, round and round in his head: 'Watch out for the Piewais, Marty. They like boys like you. They like their mums, too. And nobody tells. Nobody *ever* tells.'

03: 1979 Falling Star

Brad gives his face another dusting of powder, and leans in to check for the scar. Barely discernible. It's five years since his father's belt buckle ripped the skin beneath his eye and Mum tore up the stairs screaming for his father to stop, but it feels like yesterday.

He unhooks the gold lamé gown from its hanger and shimmies into it. Threads have pulled in places but the fabric is stiff enough that he doesn't need the Elastoplast to hide his tackle away. He jams his stockinged feet into the cork platforms. Taking the teased wig from the turned post of the dressing table, he levers it on with his fingers. It still looks more Islington deceased estate than Marilyn Monroe, but he can play with the peekaboo fringe after he's had a few drinks.

He stands back from the mirror and appraises his handiwork.

Hello Dolly.

'The cans look great,' Sid says, as Dolly descends the stairs.

'Oh shucks, Sidney.' Dolly runs her hands over her thighs and stomach to her sock-filled breasts, 'I thought you meant *my* cans.'

Sid, sitting in Mum's old recliner with a glass of bourbon and coke clutched in one hand, and a cigarette in the other, gazes at the beer can collection, newly installed on pine shelves that cover one wall of the living room.

Dolly says wistfully, 'I wish Mum had let me have them inside, they got so dusty out in the shed. No matter how carefully I washed them she'd still say she could smell the beer.'

'Would've reminded her of your dad's benders.'

'Yeah. But she never said I had to get rid of them, after we pissed him off.'

'Some women don't know when to cut their losses.'

Classic Sid, Dolly thinks. Cuts to the chase. It occurs to her that maybe Brad's never known when to cut his losses either. It's impossible to forget that blood-red rage, at sixteen, when Mum ran up the stairs to protect him, and Dad turned with that belt in his hands, and started on his mum. The old prick was still out to it, KO'd on the floor, when the police arrived courtesy of Sid, who'd called them. Later, when his father tried to crawl back into their lives, Brad had stood behind his mother at the locked screen door while she told him it was her house, and he would never step a foot back in. Through the screen wire. Brad had seen something in his father's eyes that hadn't been there before. Respect for the son who knocked him down? Fear? Dolly's never been sure, and has never quite let go of the hope that Dad might come good, despite him turning into such a prick.

Collecting beer cans was one of Dad's things. The other was going nuts for Melbourne footy. 'Worst decision of me life, coming to work in bloody Newcastle,' Dad used to moan. 'Should've stayed in Melbourne. I had a real chance of playing for the Demons.' Uncle Vin would wink and whisper, 'Wouldn't have happened, matey.'

Dad and his brother, Vin, were both boilermakers, and it had been Uncle Vin's idea to leave Victoria and to get jobs at the Steelworks, but neither of them lost their passion for watching the big men fly. Saturdays would be kicking a footy in Union Park while Mum made lunch, and afternoons glued to whatever Melbourne game was on TV. Uncle Vin used to say that Brad was a great little marker and dropped a good straight punt. Kids at school called AFL 'GayFL'. All they ever talked about was the St. George Dragons. Following the wrong code was one more difference that marked Brad as an outsider, but he'd loved those Saturdays. Dad was never the same after Uncle Vin got killed when a rack of steel-plates collapsed on him in the fabrication shop.

'That blue one with the drummer boy's me favourite,' Sid points with his cigarette.

'The Adelaide Light?' Dolly goes over and takes the can down. 'He's meant to be the bloke who founded Adelaide.'

'The jacket's stylish.'

Dolly settles in the other recliner. 'Tell me you've changed your mind about tonight, Siddy. There's still time for you to magic yourself into Lola.'

Sid shakes his head. 'Ms Lola La Bumba takes ages to dress. I'm no twenty-year-old like you. At my age it takes hours to spackle over the cracks. Anyway, I've got a bad feeling about tonight, so many people angry about the Star Hotel closing suddenly. Who knows what'll happen?'

'Oh, please, Lola,' Dolly rests her bum on the soft curved arm of Sid's chair. 'The Star's where I first saw you perform Big Spender. You outdid Shirley Bassey. You were my inspiration.'

Sid rattles the ice in his glass. 'You're just saying that so I'll change me mind, but you can forget it.'

'It's true, Sid. That was the exact moment I decided I wanted to be a drag queen.'

'Now I know you're bullshitting. You were born a drag queen. Nothing to do with me.'

Dolly gets up to replenish Sid's drink. 'Well, if flattery won't work,' she goes for the obvious, 'you'll miss a free piss-up.'

'It'll be blowflies to the honeypot,' Sid says. 'That new owner chucked us out months back and ruined a perfectly good gay bar. Why crawl back now?'

'*Please*. Just come as Sid. I ran into Kitty D'Lighter and she said Stella and the other girls will be there. They'd love to see you. I'm sure of it.'

Sid is unmoved. 'Stop asking. I'll drop you down there in the car, but you can catch a taxi home. Call that nice young taxi driver who drove us home last time. He gave you his phone number.'

Dolly hands Sid his bourbon and settles back in her chair. 'I don't know where I'd be if you didn't live next door.'

'Still in the closet wearing your ma's clothes, I expect. Certainly not the vision of beauty you are now.'

'I remember seeing Lola through the window when I was little and wondering who the beautiful lady was next door. When I asked Mum, she told me to shush and forget about it.'

'Your mum knew, but your dad was as thick as two planks. I was coming home from the club one night, and he was wandering up the street shit-faced. And he tried it on me. He almost died when I revealed me true self. I never told your mother. She had enough to contend with, and he was too drunk to remember. He called me a fucking old pervert. Pot calling kettle.'

'Poor Mum, bless her heart.'

'She was a good 'un. Rest In Peace. And that said,' Sid gets to his feet, 'I'm off to fart in peace, no disrespect intended. I'll take me drink with me. Cheers. Come over when you're ready.'

'I'll have a couple more drinks to put me in the mood,' Dolly says. 'I need to spray this wig a bit more and draw my eyebrows on. Kitty brought back this trick from her sugar-daddy trip to New York.' She moves her face to maximise the light. 'Glue-stick and lots of powder to flatten the hairs. But it takes forever to dry.

'I *was* wondering. Thought you might have gone wild and shaved them off.' Sid heads for the door. 'Righto, darl. See ya later.'

Dolly calls after him, 'Forgot to mention I might go down to Sydney. Someone's started a beer can collector's club. Feel like a day out in the Big Smoke?'

'Maybe.'

Dolly looks in the kitchen drawer for a straw. No point in ruining her lippy. Sid's never mentioned Dad hitting on Lola before. Her father claimed to hate poofters, but he'd been in the Star's middle bar plenty of times. One night he was dragged out, because he tossed his beer over Regina Vag.

He's never recognised me in drag, though, Dolly thinks. And that suits me fine. If he hit on me like he did on Lola, I'd probably king-hit him again.

Two hours and several drinks later, Dolly lets herself into Sid's, and finds him snoring in front of the blaring telly. She turns the volume down but decides not to wake him. It's only four blocks to the pub. A bit of a hike in the platforms but she'll manage.

Light blazes over the rooftops, and the racket from the Star is louder than usual, as Dolly walks along her street. She moves aside when she hears thudding footsteps behind. A man pelts past without even a look.

King Street is a shock, police cars barricade the intersection and their flashing blue lights make the crowds thronging the street beyond look surreal.

Dolly falters. Pub crowds don't worry her, but this is different.

Thousands of drinkers, and they look wild. Their noise, from only a block away, nearly drowns out the band. Perhaps Sid was right, a good night to miss. But after tonight there won't *be* a Star, and what other pub's going to put its hand up to openly welcome the drag queens and gays?

Muttering, 'There's no way you're going to be all dressed up with nowhere to go, girl,' Dolly forges on.

It takes forever to find a way through the sweating, yeasty bodies jamming Devonshire Lane. She reaches the middle bar without seeing a single face she knows. Inside is a logjam of staggering, raucous drunks, and air thick with the reek of beer, dope and vomit. There is no sign of Kitty, or Stella, or Amber, or Regina, or any of the other regular girls. No indication they've even been there.

Deflated, Dolly turns away. Straight into the path of a drunk with a wet handlebar moustache, who savagely gropes her crotch. She yelps and tries to knee him in the balls, but her lamé gown is too tight. He grabs her face and shoves his tongue down her throat. She jams her forearm against his neck but he has the suction of an octopus. He lets go only at the shout, 'Bar's closing!' joining the melee desperate to stock up on last-minute booze.

Dolly tries to push out through the crush, but she is pushed back harder and rougher. The crowd's mood is angry. A shirtless youth blotched with orange freckles screams from the shoulders of his mate, 'Stop holding out on the beer, ya cockheads, we're fucking dying for booze out here.' The crowd erupts, punches and beer cans flying in all directions. Jammed in on all sides, Dolly sees through the doors to the back bar that the Star's last act, Heroes, have climbed up into their usual place on the bar counter and are playing full throttle. When the singer cops one of the beer cans, he pauses the band and shouts over the mic for people to stop the throwing. He is met with a roar of angry boos. Randomly, he starts to sing the chorus of the Tooheys beer jingle, 'I feel like a Tooheys', and the crowd, diverted, roars along, 'I feel like a Tooheys or twoooo.' The band starts up again, only to be drowned out a minute later by a rising chant: 'Stop the pigs.'

Dolly sees the file of cops pushing towards the audio desk. The amps cut out.

In the stunned silence, someone yells, 'Pigs've pulled the fuckin' power.' Another voice roars, 'Cunts've turned off the beer.'

In the turmoil an arm snakes around Dolly's shoulder. A hand pushes roughly down her gown and into her bra. A man's voice grinds, 'Giz a feel, luv.'

Fist raised, Dolly manoeuvres to face him. But she already knows that voice. She has known it all her life.

'What the fuck is this?'

The boozy geriatric staring at the Demons footy sock dangling from his hand, is her father. Dropping the sock, he lunges for the stiff blonde curls of Dolly's wig. His snarl on his face turns to shock as he yanks it from her head.

'Leave her alone, you prick.'

Someone squeezes past Dolly and reaches for her father. The old man throws the wig at him and worms back into the crowd.

Dolly beams at the young man who hands her wig back. Brown-eyed, honey-skinned and tousle-haired, she has seen that gorgeous grin before. Leaning close, he shouts, 'Hey, remember me? From the taxi? What about we ...'

But feedback whines through the speakers, and by the time it stops, the crowd-surge has wedged Dolly and her rescuer apart. On the bar, the Heroes' singer yells 'Last song for the end of an era, the band rips into *The Star and the Slaughter*, and the city shakes to a thousand throats belting out, 'I want action. I want fighting in the streets.'

King Street is a bedlam of smoke, shrieks and careering bodies. Clutching his wig, Brad watches a man with a snake tattoo on his neck lunge-tackle a screaming woman into the gutter. Cops drag kicking drunks towards paddy wagons. A mob tries to overturn a white sedan. For a crazy moment he wants to join them, throw punches, do damage, pay back the number of times Dolly has been groped and abused, just getting this far. A man's face twists as he walks towards him. He snarls 'Move, you fucking useless piece of meat' and pushes Brad aside. Brad raises his fist to retaliate but realises what that man saw. Without the pretence of the wig, he's a stocky man wearing thick make up and a woman's tawdry gown. *The Hesperus* wrecked.

He turns away.

The roadway is a racetrack, a wrestling ring, a tip carpeted with beer cans. Missiles thread the air. Rioters kick bricks from garden walls, tear branches from trees on the median strip. Pickets are missing from the fence of Brad's mum's long-time friend, Miss Porter. He hesitates by her gate, wondering if the old woman is alright. Thongs slap the roadway. Half a dozen shirtless youths in cut-off shorts sprint towards him. Kids, barely teenagers. He freezes, hopes their impetus will carry them on to the Star.

They pass.

'Check out the fucking faggot.'

The boys have turned back. A can hits Brad's shoulder. More thud against him, not all of them empty. Hurling insults and laughing raucously, the kids come closer. Brad grabs hold of a picket, reefs it from the fence and raises it like a baseball bat.

Whoomph.

Brad feels the explosion as more sensation than noise. As if the air has thickened and pushed against him.

The youths take off, charging towards the column of flame erupting from a police van. A mob-howl, jubilant and primal, rolls down the street like a wave.

Brad leans over the picket fence and gasps for breath. He wills himself not to cry.

The howl diminishes. He hears a voice shout his name.

Backlit by the street's surreal flare, a man staggers towards him. Brad doesn't need light though, to recognise that barrel shape, those skinny bow-legs. For a heart-stopping moment he wonders if his father has come to his rescue. Then the years of hurt hit like a punch to the guts. Fists clenched, he roars, 'Any closer, and this time I'll knock your bloody head off.'

Brad's father stops ten metres away. Without a word, he steadies himself and extends his arms. Something falls from his hands as his foot swings forward.

Brad watches the shape sail into the air. Thinking, no one can do this in four-inch platforms, he leaps for the mark. He could be Alex Jesaulenko or Billy Picken or Peter Moore, or any of the great, beautiful, streamlined high flyers of the AFL.

Something hard and cylindrical thwacks into his palms.

Miscalculating his landing, he goes down in a heap.

'Jesus wept.'

Brad lifts his gaze from the can nestled in the wig on his lap to see pink felt slippers and heavily veined ankles beneath a maroon quilted dressing gown.

Sid leans down to help him to his feet.

'Are you alright, Doll? Come on, let's get you home. I'm sorry, darl, I let you down tonight. Went to sleep in me chair. Didn't hear you come in. Should never have let you do this on your own. Here, give me that,' he reaches for the wig, 'Would you like a hand to put it back on?'

'Forget it Sid, I don't need it now.'

Brad stuffs the wig down the front of his dress into the space vacated by the lost footy sock.

Sid laughs. 'That must feel like a funnel web spider scrabbling round in there.'

Brad smiles ruefully.

Holding each other for support they negotiate the roadway debris. Brad pulls away under the first unbroken streetlight to peer at the beer can. Its logo is a tank-shaped bird with skinny legs. He reads aloud, 'EMU EXPORT LAGER, THE SWAN BREWERY Co. LTD. OF PERTH WEST AUSTRALIA 13 FL OZ.

'Sid! It's a full Bush Chook! A steel can, hardly a dent. The real deal.'

'Nice. You don't already have this one, darl?'

'No way. Steel Emus are rare as hen's teeth.'

'Lucky you found it in that chaos.'

'I didn't find it, Sid. My dad gave it to me. Sort of.'

'You saw that old bastard, and he gave you something?' Sid sniffs. 'That's a turn up for the books. Where would he've got it?'

'Probably nicked it from the trophy cans, behind the Star's front bar.'

'Wouldn't be at all surprised.'

'He groped me, too, Sid. In the back bar. I wanted to kill him. Then he turned up here and kicked this at me. A proper footy punt, and I took the mark. What was that about? To prove that I'm useless, or did he want me to catch it?

'Just a fucking old drunk. Count it as a win, darl. Stick it in your collection. Pride of place.'

Brad shakes his head. 'I'm done with the cans, Sid. Collecting was that prick's idea, not mine. I kept it going for him, but what the fuck for?'

'So what do you reckon it's worth?'

Brad stares. 'Could be a bit, I reckon.'

'Photograph it.' Sid takes Brad's arm again. 'Photograph every one of them, darl. Show those collectors when we go down to Sydney. You might find a buyer. And while we're down there, we could hit Kings Cross. I'll take you to me favourite wig shop.'

04: 1989 Demolition

Bess calls Lena to say she feels shattered, there is still packing to do, and she can't possibly make it to the party.

Lena replies, 'Liz, darling, I won't hear of it. *Everyone* feels that way about the earthquake, though we were *so* lucky not having much damage up here, on The Hill. But it's New Year's Eve, and *somebody* has to celebrate, it's almost a duty. And it's also our send-off for *you*. A sabbatical in Cambridge, for an entire year! Everyone will move *mountains* to say goodbye, and if some sadly can't get here, then small and intimate will be perfect, won't it? For your last night?'

Bess, gazes at the disorder of her apartment, and sighs. 'If I can get a taxi. But I'll be late.'

'Late we can manage, but I can't miss a last hug. Things to do, Liz, have to rush.'

'Wait! Lena?'

Replacing the beeping receiver, Bess wonders bleakly why she always leaves everything to the last-minute. She wanted to ask about Bax, but of course he'll be coming. There might be phone lines down all across Newcastle and streets blocked in the city centre, but he'll be the one moving mountains.

Small and intimate, Bess thinks, as she arrives to a barrage of music and hilarity that feels like an assault.

Lena pushes through the crush to rescue her. 'Darling! It's nearly *eleven*! But you're here! Tonight has become so much bigger than we expected. Neighbours without power, people having to change plans, some bringing marooned friends and family.'

From a quieter spot at the back of the room, they watch Cliff's small, neat form weave through the crowd, three champagne coupes and a bottle clutched high in the air.

'Liz! I was beginning to think we'd lost you. Champers, my dear?' He grins. 'I saved you the Moët.'

Handing over the glasses, he pops the cork and pours. Lifting his brimming coupe, he offers his well-worn toast, 'to Marie Antoinette's breasts.' With an appreciative glance at Bess, he adds, 'And of course to you, Liz, for a rewarding sabbatical. Wonderful dress, darling. I must say, if it had been you modelling for these coupes, they'd be far more generous.'

Mellowed by several quickly-downed drinks, Bess raids the drinks tub for a cold-beaded bottle of Moët and two clean glasses, and exits the party room. Breathing heavily, she props herself against the corridor wall and frowns.

Too noisy, and too many people. Unexpected people. One, particularly unexpected.

Pushing that thought away, she pictures Bax, standing tall and handsome in the crowd, his face tanned, blond hair gleaming. She smiles: I was coming straight to you, my love, but that young Classics tutor, grabbing my hand, so expected, and pulling me into the middle of the dance floor. Me, jiving, and everybody watching! But wasn't it fun? And you watching me, Bax, were you surprised? So hard to plan things, I tried and tried to call you, but with half the city's phones out—it doesn't matter now because we are both here for my last night, and I saw your special nod. So here I am, my love, escaped from the madding crowd.

But Bax doesn't emerge. Realising it might not be the best thing to wait for him where people come and go, Bess decides, I'll go ahead, Bax. But you'll know where to find me. Just don't take too long.

She wanders, somewhat unsteady in her stilettoes, down the familiar hallway. The last time she dropped by, Cliff had brought her out here to show off his latest acquisitions. Two impressive photographs by Max Dupain. One of giant coal-loader cranes at the docks, rearing over Lilliputian men, the other of coal ships berthed along the Hunter, waiting for their cargo. Every detail clear, right down to the depth calibrations on the ship's hulls. She looks out for the photos but she has forgotten exactly where they were and the hallway light is too strangely dim to pick them out from the other works hanging. Remembering how Cliff had said, proudly, 'The might of industrial Newcastle,' she wonders uneasily, what would you say now, Cliffie, after so much of our city has collapsed around us?

The overhead lights flicker. Bess hurries on to the door with brass plate inscribed *Guest Powder Room*. It usually gleams under the hall lights, but now looks so dull she can hardly read it. She knocks. No answer, Tentatively, she pushes the door, and falters, seeing the darkness within. Heart pounding, she gropes for the switch. Light blasts the room to its familiar glassy spaciousness, gleaming white marble, glass and mirrors reflecting and refracting.

The party noise mutes as she closes the door. Latching it, she presses her hot cheek to its cool painted surface ad breathes, '*Peace*.'

Turning towards the vanity, Bess stops short at the sight of a big crack running vertically up the mirror with a branch to the side, like a leaning tree. She gasps. The earthquake? But Lena said not much damage. Shaking her head to clear it, she moves further along the benchtop. After carefully positioning the coupes, she studies them for a moment. Deciding that Bax is on his way, there's no point in letting the Moët get warm, she pops the champagne with a little scream. Pouring an ample glassful she raises the coupe to her reflection. 'To you, clever girl, and to grand adventures.'

The woman who toasts her back has eyes exotically lined with kohl, lips that are generously crimsoned, and over-sized gold hoops hanging from her ears. Her deep red curls tumble to the plunging shawl collar of her emerald satin dress. Her edges are rounded. Her skin is luminous.

'Not bad for thirty-eight.'

Pouting at the mirror, Bess strikes a Marilyn Monroe pose,.shoulders curved to accentuate her generous cleavage. She tilts too far. As she grabs the vanity for support, she sees her shawl collar slip from one shoulder, one breast nearly spill from its cup. Too close to the glass, she finds her reflection less kind, damp hair stuck to her flushed face, her lipstick seeping into tiny cracks. Her dress is blotched with perspiration.

'Damn. Bit of a wreck.'

Straightening, she says sternly to her reflection, 'Madam, you are disheveled.' The woman smiles back and winks, 'So I am. Give me a moment, and I'll *shevel* myself.'

Shevel. Bess throws back her head and laughs. So funny, must tell Bax. But the mirror shows too many teeth in that laughing mouth, and her mirth falters.

She looks to her wristwatch for the time, and is confused to find that she isn't wearing it, although there is the pale patch of its shape against her tan. Mum's watch. I've worn since she died. What have I done with it?

An image comes sharply to her mind of the small rectangular watch-face glass shattered, and the fine black hands flattened at 10:28. Her throat constricts.

Bax, where are you? Why am I leaving you?

She moves away from the mirror, leaning back to the marble-tiled coolness of a wall and the memory of their first meeting. He had entered the faculty common room, tall and slender, shining straw-coloured hair down to his collar, nodded to the colleagues chatting by the tea urn, and walked directly to where she stood by the window. He'd extended his hand.

'John Dunn, contemporary American lit and general all-rounder. New *bloke* on staff, apparently. Whatever *bloke* represents.'

He stood close in the American way, his grasp firm and warm. A million-dollar smile. Hazel eyes that saw too much.

Reluctantly detaching from his grip, she'd said, 'Liz. Elizabeth Shand, metaphysical poets and also general all-rounder. And I'm sorry, but you can't be.'

He'd raised an eyebrow. 'A bloke? Or an all-rounder?'

'John Donne. I already have one in my life—four years of a Doctorate dedicated to him. How can I possibly fit in another?'

'Donne?' His smile crooked up at the corners. 'That old sermoniser, why choose him?'

'No-one but Donne has ever made religion so erotic.'

The memory of his laugh still makes her feel wrapped in fur.

The first time she called him Johnny, he said, 'My wife is the only person who calls me that,' and, for a moment, Bess was unsure whether she was on forbidden ground, or if he'd thrown down a gauntlet. The answer was already irrelevant, their connection so inevitable and electric it took her breath away. Later, teasing him with Jack, Jock, Jonno, Giacomo and more, he had succumbed, saying, 'Why can't you Australians cope with a given name? You choose, Queen Bess. I surrender.'

So, I did. I wormed from you that your christened name was Baxter, and promised I would make you love the first half of it, at least. The plot was set, secret names, the pretense of fiction, concealment from the start. What else can you do when you fall for someone so instantly and completely?

Through the door, Bess hears a surge of music on the stereo. Adam Ant singing, *goody two, goody two, goody goody two shoes,* she does a wobbly twirl. Wine sloshes from the shallow coupe over her fingers. She swipes her tongue at the trickle running down her wrist, Stupid coupes! Give me a flute any day. It's a pity the earthquake didn't smash the lot.

But thinking again of the earthquake rocks her. She quickly downs her champagne, she pours another, and diverts her thoughts to jiving. Laughing, she sways into a triple-step and, at the point of realising that it doesn't work without the counterbalance of a partner, thinks, I need you, classics guy! Euan, Evan? British accent, Welsh? Not bad looking, and a terrific mover! Who'd've guessed? Like a shadow in the faculty all year. Not my style! I was sassy as hell when I came on staff. Sassy enough for you, Bax, right from the start.

Bax. She can't wait to bury her face in his chest, draw in the warm, sweet musk of him, undo all his buttons one by one. But my face! The state of it!

She swings to the mirror to check her makeup, runs her fingers along her lip line and beneath the smudged kohl, pulls her collar back into place, and swears when her fingers leave black smears on the satin. Wetting the corner of a hand towel, she tries unsuccessfully to rub the marks off. As she fumbles to tuck the stains out of sight, she notices her breast is mottled with purple. Alarmed, she pushes the collar further down. Her shoulder and upper arm are patchworked mauve and indigo. Pressing one of the patches, she winces. Instinctively, she slides her hand from hip to thigh over green satin, anticipating the map of pain her fingers meet.

How could I not know this?

Hazily she remembers searching for a dress. *This* dress, with its big shawl collar that can hide so much. She had rummaged through her suitcases, and the boxes she'd locked in the spare bedroom because of the incoming tenant, finding it, finally, hanging under a coat in the cupboard. When the taxi that she'd booked honked in the street, she had flung the dress on and rushed out the door still fixing her earrings, leaving clothes strewn everywhere behind her and her suitcases splayed like shot birds.

Anxiety flutters in Bess's chest. She needs to go home. Repack it all before her sister and niece arrive at six in the morning to drive her to Sydney. Ten-year-old Cassie has been excited for weeks at the thought of waving Aunt Lizzie off in a big plane at the airport. Have to ring Mai. Ask her to come earlier. Help me to sort out the mess.

But when she raises her eyes, mirror-Bess says, 'You know they're not taking you. Why would they? You were vicious. You screamed at Mai, "Don't bother driving me. I'll take the train down." Cassie in tears. The distress on Mai's face.'

That was how I said goodbye?

Bess leans back against the vanity, wraps her arms around herself and rocks miserably. You know all of my secrets, Mai. You and Cass are the core of me. Why did I do that to you?'

'All your eggs in one basket.'

That's what Mai said. That's what started the fight. Feminist Mai, who's always set her own terms. Who embraced single motherhood, graduated in psychology at fifty.

Her throat tightening, Bess remembers calling her sister a hypocrite. Spitting back at her, 'Where did that come from, Mai? You advocate for choice, but not for your *sister*? You knew about Bax from the start. He was *my* choice, to love who I want, on *my* terms. No guilt. No strings. *All your eggs in one basket*? What sort of psychologist would say *that* to a woman?' And Mai, hurrying Cassie out Bess's front door, had shouted over her shoulder, 'Isn't it the real reason you are taking off to Cambridge, Liz? Bax won't change. Why would he? Has he even once asked you to stay? A new start before you're forty, *you've* said that. Please don't give up on it now.'

Bess doubles over and wails. Because there *are* strings, and all of them Bax's. His wife, his kids, the job and house and lifestyle he wants. 'And no baby for me, Bax. I did want your baby. I would have pretended it wasn't yours. But you always said no.'

Salt trickles into the corner of her mouth. Swiping her face with the back of her hand, she pushes the thought of a child away. Closing her eyes, she succumbs again to memories of Bax. So many stolen moments, and every one of them worth it: those first delirious months with him, sex hot and fast in his car and university storerooms, the first bliss of lying naked against him at the Tudor Inn, laughing deliriously when he asked, 'Am I falling for a cheapskate?'

The anonymity of cheap hotels had a frisson that sucked them both in.

Bess hears a click. The bathroom door is opening.

'Bax?'

'Whoops.' A woman's voice. 'It's unlocked. Sorry, didn't realise.'

'I might be a while!'

Bess holds her breath as the door shuts. Surely I locked it? 'Silly *moi*. Anyone could have barged in.'

Champers in hand, and willing her stilettoes to behave, she crosses the glossy floor. She pushes the knob on the privacy latch across. It refuses to engage. She jiggles, pushes harder. No difference. Frustrated, she takes another gulp from her coupe and carefully sets it on the floor beside her. She studies the latch closely. The tongue doesn't appear to align with the keeper, as if the door has twisted. She straightens, and manages to coordinate a thrust of her hip with jabbing the latch hard. She gives a satisfied laugh as the tongue slides home.

Shaking the pain from her hand, she returns to the mirror and confides to her reflection, 'Shouldn't have come tonight. But Bax! And he's here! But not here with me! I would've stayed dancing if I'd known you'd take this long.'

She paces in the confined space. Stopping by the toilet, she bunches the slippery folds of her dress, pulls down her knickers, and regally sits. The room's slick surfaces amplify the tinkling sound as she pees. *Tinkling*, she giggles. The coy euphemism of all the *nice* girls at high school. 'Oh, hang on,' she mimics, 'I just need a *tinkle*! But none of that stupidity for you and me, Lena. We were the feisty ones, ready to take on the world. Yet here we are, both still in Newcastle. You weathered the scandal of the little Prof and his lissome undergrad lover, half his age, and now you're Faculty Head, with your Vice Chancellor husband, big house on The Hill, and more overseas vacations than either of you can count.

And me?

Forlornly, Bess pictures her last crop of students as they straggled in to her first poetry lecture. One hour to win them or to watch their eyes glaze over for good. And win them she did, always, she makes certain of that. But the effort to keep making sure of that outcome, of bringing freshness to each new lecture and tutorial, is staring to wear.

Tinkling, she thinks again. Why not use that to kick off next Monday's lecture! Tinkling, and onomato*pee*ia. A frisson of naughtiness to sit them all up. After which I shall announce my new literary term: *onomato-euphemism*.

Laughing, she wipes and flushes. But, restoring her knickers and dress, she remembers that the last university term is over. It is already weeks into the holiday break. What am I thinking? Tomorrow is 1990. No more students, or lectures, Newcastle Donne and dusted, I'm flying off to Cambridge. Party time!

But a whole year without Bax?

Her euphoria shrivels like a touched snail.

Elbows propped on the vanity, Bess slumps until her forearms and cheek rest against the cool marble. Three days ago, she and Bax sprawled naked on a rumpled bed in the Kent Hotel. The tall casement windows of their room were open to the balcony and the breeze from Beaumont Street filled the room with warmth. Languidly, she'd turned in his arms and reached to the dark-varnished bedside table to check her watch. Ten-twenty. Bax was on a promise to be home by eleven to help prepare lunch for holiday guests, and he needed to be convincingly sweaty from his bike ride. Rising from the bed, Bess stood for a moment to absorb how the buttery light gilded the sweat-sheen on Bax's back and buttocks. She had leant to him and murmured, 'Except you enthral me, never shall be free. Nor ever chaste, except you ravish me.'

Opening one eye, Bax said with a lazy smile, 'Wasn't Donne talking about purity?'

'He was. Pure is how you make me feel.'

Pulling on her summer frock, Bess reminded him that it was nearly time to leave. 'I'm just ducking to the loo. I'll be back in a minute, don't go without me.' She ran along the dim corridor to the bathroom, her golden lover shining in her mind.

Bess opens her eyes to the harsh brightness of the guest bathroom. Her mouth tastes sour. Reaching for the Moët bottle she swigs awkwardly, wine spilling from her mouth. Dismayed by the stain spreading across green satin, she tries to blot the wetness with a towel. This is *your* fault, Bax. That wouldn't have happened if you were here. Christ, you're taking so long. Do I have to come and get you?

But panic surges at the thought of leaving that bright ensuite, and going back along that dim corridor, to the room with all the people who had stared at her crazy dancing. And that woman beside you, laughing, Bax. Laughing at me. Why is she here? You've always said that your wife hates university parties. Why bring her? Tonight, of all nights?

Rat-tat-tat-tat-tat. Somebody is knocking at the door.

Bess draws a breath. Bax?

Rat-tat-tat, Rat-tat-tat-tat-TAT.

The knocking becomes banging. A man's voice shouts, 'Is somebody in there? Hello? *Hello*?'

Bess freezes. That's not *your* voice, Bax. Why isn't it *your* voice?

A pulse starts to pound in her head.

Suddenly, the knocking is overtaken by another blast of music. The party stereo turned up full to a song already heard once, tonight. The song they shouldn't be playing. Bess shrinks at the staccato beat of hammering piano keys, *DadaDah DadaDah DadaDAHdadadada*, and Carole King's reedy voice singing, 'I feel the earth ... move ... under my feet'. Party guests are stomping their feet in response. Bess feels the floor reverberate. her head fills with the roar of 'I feel the sky tumbling down, tumbling down'. When the music just as suddenly mutes, she is screaming, 'Turn it off. *TURN IT OFF.*'

Drawing a breath, she hears the man in the corridor shout, 'For Chrisssake stop yelling! Just unlock the damn door.'

Why can't you be Bax, Bess thinks as, hand clamped over her mouth, she watches the door handle jerk.

Another voice calls, 'Liz, are you in there? Are you alright? Can you come out? Please, say something.'

Bess sags with relief. Lena. Who came through those judging faces. You put your arms around me, Lena, and told everyone that I was right. You made someone take that horrible record off the stereo. Because of the earthquake, you said. Because people are suffering in this town.

'*I'm* suffering, Lena,' she whimpers.

'Liz, darling, we need you to help us celebrate. Please come and join us. It's almost midnight.'

Midnight? Bess scrambles up from the floor, calling wildly, 'I'm coming Lena. But awful, awful mess. Need to clean up.' Turning back to the mirror, she slips on the shiny tiles. She feels her ankle twist, the stiletto heel snap. Angrily she bends to take the shoe off, and throws it across the room. Something shatters.

Shards of Cliff's champagne coupe scatter across the tiles.

'Fuck,' Bess wails. 'Marie Antoinette's breast!'

Looking back at her reflection, acid rises in her throat. The vision is horrifying. Distorted by the mirror's long, branching crack, her face looks split down the middle: half of her mouth is where her chin should be, one eye is on her cheek, a section of her head is missing. Grinding, wrenching sounds thunder through her brain, and she is back in the Kent Hotel's claustrophobic brown-tiled bathroom cubicle, the walls shuddering, the floor buckling like cardboard beneath her feet. She'd grabbed hold of the pink porcelain basin for support, but it jerked from her grasp and she was falling, her shoulder and hip blasting into pain. Huddled in pitch darkness, her hands pressed to her ears, there was no way to block the roar of reality tearing apart. When most of the noises had stopped, leaving the building twitching like a dying animal, she'd climbed shakily to her feet and kicked and clawed at the wedged cubicle door until she managed to drag it open, then she ran, along the surreal obstacle course of the listing dark corridor, into the room where she'd left Bax, the door already open revealing the double bed at an impossible angle on the slanting floor and the wooden table and chair upended. Beyond, in the dust-swirling brightness, she saw the entire front wall of the room with its wafting curtains and high casement windows they'd made love in, and the balcony beyond, all gone. Bax, gone.

Screaming for him, Bess had dropped to her knees and crawled down the shuddering incline of the floor. But the screams from outside were louder, the sound of sirens louder. When she reached the edge, she saw the apocalypse, Beaumont Street covered in smashed beams, twisted iron and broken masonry, dust-covered people running away, others in cartoon-bright clothes pouring out of the shopfronts. Directly below her, men shouted as they strained to lift a section of the collapsed balcony. Others, kneeling on the rubble, tried to pull something out from beneath.

Opening her eyes to Cliff and Lena's blazing white powder room, Bess can't stop her howl of despair as she re-lives watching that crumpled shape emerging from the rubble. The howl that continued as she crawled back up the canting floor, past the bed where she'd left Bax drowsing, past the bedside table where he'd put his wallet, past the shoes and clothes he had left lying on the floor, all of it gone. Howling because Bax hadn't fallen into the street below. He had fled without her.

The man out in the corridor shouts for a screwdriver. Bess crawls towards the door, her face wet with tears, but she has finished screaming. Something crunches beneath her hand. Glass from Cliffie's coupe. She watches the blood pool in her palm before crawling on. Reaching the door she rises to her knees and pulls down on the handle.

'That's no help,' the man in the corridor bellows. 'Slide the damn privacy latch back.'

Bess does what he asks, but her bloodied fingers keep slipping. The howling is back in her head. The walls are closing in. Pounding her fists against the glossy white door, she knows she will never get out.

05: 2003 Closure

June 14, 2003. Here you go again, levering yourself into the Camira and driving out to Kooragang. To witness BHP being wiped from the face of Newcastle. To watch the steelmaking shed fall the way that you fell, nearly a decade ago.

Like they say in the movies: it's payback time. Witnessing is for gloating.

There's the usual traffic bottleneck after the Tourle Street Bridge: a chance to check out the solitary black swan on the tidal lagoon, and the slow-turning wind turbine opposite. It has to be true that renewables will be the future, but that giant windmill seems as effective as a dandelion seed-head, once the meccano of loading infrastructure and five-storey coal mounds come into view beyond it. Four coal ships, moored along the wharf, swallow ton after ton of the stinking stuff.

In the rear-view, you see cars are pulling off the road. You hear the siren, follow their lead. The Cami creeps along the shoulder and into the shadow of the overhead coal conveyor which is funneling an infinite stream of fossil fuel profits towards ever-yawning corporate pockets.

When an ambulance passes, there is always that sense of dread.

Anxiety stays leaden in your gut as the traffic crawls on. You could forget the industrial dystopia and swing left at the roundabout. Soar over Stockton Bridge and take in the view of Nobbys Lighthouse. Watch terns lift off the tidal marsh beside Fullerton Cove as you hoon down towards Stockton Spit and the hard blue of the Tasman Sea. Keep driving up to Nelson Bay, park above Fingal Beach, look out to the islands, absorb the serenity.

But today isn't about escape. It's about reckoning.

You stay on Kooragang, the island that never was, hook a right at the roundabout and enter the realm of sky-eating derricks and conveyors, steel silos, rusting machinery, cyclone fences, locked gates, dead weeds and dust.

You remember Nige telling your that Kooragang means 'place

of many birds'. There are streets named Cormorant, Heron, Egret, Sandpiper and sure as hell there'll be one named Seagull somewhere. Someone with a fine sense of irony named the streets around here, because, apart from the seagulls, and an occasional swan on the strip-lagoon, most self-respecting birds would've left decades ago. Back when the developers began dumping fill into the creeks and the swamps to amalgamate the islands, turning the once-pristine river delta into an industrial wasteland.

The barricade of corrugated iron buildings opens to an undeveloped stretch beside the south arm of the Hunter. You follow the tracks to where other cars are already parked. There's no knowing what rubbish the weeds conceal, and the Cami's slung low. Some men huddle against the cold in folding aluminium chairs, video cameras set up on tripods, or prop their bums against their car bonnets, but most sit in their vehicles. Heads turn as you pass, some faces familiar, but not who you are looking for. Bert Sparkes. Sparkie. You see him taking a folding chair from the boot of his car. More gaunt and stooped, and his bald head covered by a wide-brimmed hat, but you'd recognise him anywhere. He glances around as you pass and gives the slightest nod, which you return in kind. Neither of you are here to socialise.

You drive past the last vehicle, a reversed-in F100 with four beefy guys crammed in the tray around a huge Esky who must reckon they'rre in the dress circle. Fifteen metres further on you nose the Cami towards the brown river, pull on the handbrake, cut the engine, and sit.

Downstream a few stunted mangroves interrupt the city view, but that's not the view which interests you. You stare across the broad south channel to the Steelworks—now ex-Steelworks—the decaying carcass of a beast that consumed too many lives, one way or another.

Perspective does strange things. The width of the choppy river and five years of dismantling make the BHP site and a century of manic industrial activity look irrelevant. Without the iron walls rising like skyscrapers, and the relentless rumble of so-called progress, and the pollution that congealed in your nostrils and the back of your throat and dirtied your skin, what's left looks like a jaw full of broken stumps.

The past poised to fall over the edge of memory.

But it refuses to. The steaming warren of production you walked into, every rostered day for three years, is still with you. Memories of the searing heat of the furnaces and the stink of toxic fumes being sucked into the extraction hoods, the groaning, hissing and rumbling still moil in your mind.

The river-glitter hurts your eyes. Ferreting a pair of sunnies from the glovebox, you put them on and continue staring at the massive grey shed that dominates the wasteland opposite. It strikes you that the towers of blast furnace 3 and 4, which flank it on either side, look like goalposts waiting for the big one.

That goal goes through today.

You reach into the back seat, fumble for the tartan rug, and groan like an old timer as you tuck it around your legs. Thirty-four isn't old. You were nineteen when you became an electrical apprentice at the Steelworks. 1988. Australia's bicentennial and the year the Newcastle Knights joined the New South Wales Rugby League. It felt like you were part of history. The induction tour through the different workshops and departments was conducted by a lantern-jawed worker, who finished under the old arch with *PROUD TO BE THE BEST* written in steel. 'You recruits would be fools to waste this opportunity,' he said. 'BHP offers jobs for life. There is an Electrical Recruit of the Year Award, and every one of you should aim for it.'

Grinning at that steel motto like a dork, you determined you would take out that award. Show everyone.

Winning it did you no favours.

Everything about the Works overwhelmed you that first year. The sheer size of the site with its train lines and roads, the hordes of people constantly changing shifts. You were a drone among thousands, working to keep the industrial queen endlessly churning out iron and steel. Maybe everyone felt that at the start, but you never got over it.

You discovered the power of the list. Pocket notebooks filled with rules to be learnt, techniques to master, OH&S regulations, union directives, dangers to be aware of, the jobs to be done, points to check off to ensure they were done properly. You also listed things you were good at:

Learning fast
Retaining information
Mastering techniques
Taking orders
Making connections (electrical pun-alert)
Thinking things through
Being methodical
Checking and re-checking
Looking after the tools
TAFE coursework, paperwork, reports (being literate gave an edge)
Spatial awareness
Keeping things tidy and clean
Keeping fit
List making
OH&S.
Yes, fuck it, OH&S! And on that note:
Turning a blind eye

Nothing much seems to be happening over on the site. You open the car window a crack. A faint rumble spills in with the cold air. When that shed collapses, you want to hear it.

You shiver. Should have worn a warmer jacket. The weight you've stacked on is no insulator.

'KEEP FIT.' That list filled a notebook. Gym times, exercise routines, stuff to wear, eat, drink. Strength was the only way to cope with the job's physicality. You might be stuffed by the end of each day, but you'd still go to the gym or run. You muscled up. Took to wearing singlet tops to the pub.

It was your toned body that lured Belle, that Friday night at the Carrington.

You were at the bar with Groper and Nige, bored by their endless-loop discussion about the Knights' disappointing first season, their ignoble finish near the bottom of the ladder. When the excuses ran out, they rehashed the Men-of-Steel's glorious Herald Challenge pre-season win over the reigning premiers, the Sea Eagles. You'd leant back against the bar and idly surveyed the room. Not exactly idly. You'd noticed her as soon as you walked in, the stand-out in a group of four sharp looking women. Her small waist, full breasts, black hair sculpted close to her head, silver looped through her ears, more on her fingers. You'd turned away as she approached the bar, not wanting to look like a perve. She came close enough for the hair on your arms to prickle, and ordered a round for her table. Strong nose, long throat. She'd turned and propped her elbow on the bar to give you the benefit of her intense blue eyes, killer smile, creamy cleavage.

'That's a fine-looking bicep. Can I touch it?'

The lists drove Belle mad, finding them all over your flat. She introduced you to her friends as her obsessive-compulsive lover, which always got a laugh, and prying into which parts of her you were most OC about.

That warm clinging body was the one soft thing in your life.

Her body, at least, was soft.

Dust sheets sideways in the air as an excavator moves into place. You know there will be at least two, tensioning the cables so the demo team can cut key structural points to destabilise the building.

A controlled collapse.

That's what should happen.

It doesn't always. Nine months back, someone stuffed up the calculations on a boiler demo. It collapsed on five workers: two badly injured, one poor bastard crushed under tons of steel. Before that, a young boilermaker on a cherry-picker, cutting the last perforations on an ore-bridge, had to leap for his life as the whole fucking structure came down around him.

You shiver, pull the rug higher. Is that why you're here? In case there's another accident? That relief of seeing something bad happen at the site, and not being involved? There but for the grace?

The problem with grace is it's selective, but your psychologist reckons that thinking through your fascination with accidents will help the healing process.

A crane skims low above the water. They have always been one of your favourite birds. There used to be a lot around here, elegant blue-grey shapes stalking the paddocks and river shallows. It still strikes you, every time you see the giant ore-bridge cranes, how much they look like their namesakes. Dad laughed every time you said, as a kid, that you wanted to see the ore-bridge cranes fly.

It was funny how unimpressed he was when you applied for the apprenticeship. He knew how everything industrial fascinated you. When you started at the Works, you thought he'd look out for you, but you hardly ever crossed paths. If you swung by the blast furnaces to say gidday, he'd look uncomfortable. By then the bosses were starting to cut back the workforce and your dad was one of the loudest about refusing a severance package. A cop-out he said. He planned to work until he dropped or the Company made him stop. But right after your accident he took the payout and walked. Bought himself a fibro at Dudley, and signed the Cooks Hill home over to you. He's a twenty-minute drive away but you only see him once or twice a year, and he's never been one to phone.

Belle walked too, after the accident.

Stupidly you'd thought it was love, but face it, she was a babe on the prowl and moving on was always on the cards.

At first, the lists of names helped sort out your co-workers. Visual memory prompts like 'limps' or 'broken tooth' or 'joker' beside each name. Nicknames dominated the culture. Recruits were called names like Teabag, Nipper, or Gofer, to reinforce their lackey status. You'd know a co-worker's nickname well before you learnt their actual name, and often, as you got to know the person, the nickname made perfect sense. Blaster's vile flatulence, Speedy moving nowhere fast. You'd assumed that Groper was a sleaze, before discovering that the Gropers were a Nelson Bay rugby club. When you asked if he was from up that way, he'd laughed, 'Nah, those Gropers are named for a bloody fish. I'm a Sandgroper original, from WA.'

During lunchbreaks Nige quietly explained the names you didn't get. 'Needle, because he's a prick. Nobby 'cos he's always out past Nobbys fishing. Bilbo? Dunno, but I heard he's had it from school, hairy toes maybe. Pony's a show pony, always styling up his hair, Bags is a showbag—full of crap. Duck, well that's obvious, isn't it? Feet too close to his bum—he's got duck's disease.' You asked about Spider. Nige flicked a disdainful glance at the sweaty looking middle-aged man on the far side of the room: 'Believe me, you don't want to know.'

It was a game of double-guessing. Who to be wary of, who to trust. Some men inhabited their persona. Like Jackknife, who was small, angular and vicious. Maybe being nasty made him feel safe. Everyone has their defences.

Nige's self-protection involved putting up with his nickname, 'Nigg'. A Worimi man from Forster, he'd done his apprenticeship with a cousin up at Tweed Heads and played rugby with the Seagulls. When talk started about Newcastle joining the New South Wales Rugby League, he'd come back down to follow his dream: play with the Newcastle Knights. He never made it. The talent pool was too bloody big, he said, and he was probably getting a bit old. He would have been around thirty back then. Nige still had an athlete's body, and after you and he passed each other a few times, jogging around the suburbs after work, he suggested running together. You'd never felt comfortable calling him Nigg, which seemed blatantly racist. He grinned when you told him that. 'Oh, yeah, workplace humour, *a bit of word-play*, though when you've been lumbered with 'Nigel', Nigg sounds sort of okay. I handle it. I'm different enough already for these blokes, without having a name that sets me apart as well.'

You already knew about difference. From the start you introduced yourself as Nat, trusting your lean, androgynous build and David Bowie quaff to help you fit in. It might have worked on paper, but using that name as a shield on the factory floor had a snowball's hope in hell of success. The nicknames accumulated fast, ranging from Bowie, Natrat and Batty Natty to the apparently hilarious, Batshit, Ratshit, or Natshit, while your build earned you names like Streak, and the optimistic Streaker. Overt discussions on topics like boobs being strapped down with tyre tube, and pranks, such as the two mouldy rockmelons in a triple D bra that you found one morning hung from the handle of your locker, maintained the incessant misogyny.

Homophobia was also rife. One break, as Nige sat down beside you, Ferret (obvious similarity) yelled, 'No point tryin', mate, though maybe y'like her because she looks like a boy? Sure ya not a faggot?'

Nige shot back, 'Nah, mate, but looking at your pretty face I wish I was.'

The other men in the room cracked up. Ferret copped 'Pretty Boy' chirped in budgie-voices after that.

Maybe you should have kept a list of things you weren't good at.

Predicting people

Keeping clean

Keeping Belle

At first Belle had got off on that metallic, tarry Works smell which never left no matter how much you shampooed, scrubbed and scented. Like animal scent, she said. Months later, lying in bed without touching, you'd forced a laugh and mentioned blokes at work who claimed their women stayed hot for that smell of soap and industry.

She didn't comment.

Those blokes were wankers.

Maybe Belle was right, about you being OC.

The first list of co-workers morphed into a hefty notebook, names embellished with exclamation marks, heavy underlining, black circles. Notes became paragraphs, pages.

'Ageist. Sexist.' You wrote that the day Bert Sparkes called you Girlie. Though you scribbled it out when it dawned that the other recruits copped similar infantilising, like Lad, Young'un, Son, Matey. Soon there was a star beside Bert's name. A long-time union rep and collective bargaining advocate, he trained new workers properly as a point of honour, and held BHP in high regard. 'The Company made this town,' he'd say. 'Without it we'd be nowhere.'

Circulating employees through different sections was standard Company procedure and you began to look forward to rosters with Sparkie. Tall, with slightly bowed shoulders and thinning hair, he was old school, one of the few supervisors in the hierarchy still happy to answer questions and explain process. A decent man, but hopeless at remembering names. You found out he planned to nominate you for a first-year apprentice award when he waved the form at you, saying, 'Tell me your name again, Girlie.'

When you won, the general perception was of BHP slapping itself on the back. 'Female Apprentice Wins' made a good headline.

Later, during the court case, the QC for the Defence argued that nicknames were part of the 'comradely culture' at the Works. 'Creating a sense of *bonhomie*', he said, smugly. In response your lawyer, Maggie Olsen, read out from your notebooks the long list of names you'd been called, adding, 'I suggest, Your Honour, that nicknames such as Puss, Twat, Snatch, Minge, Target, Rapebait and Breakfast, suggest *active* aggression rather than 'bonhomie'.'

Names that made Bert's 'Girlie' seem like a courtesy.

You had braced yourself against every second word in any given conversation being 'cunt', and ignored the centrefolds of spread legs and Hindenburg tits—torn from *Penthouse* and *Playboy*, and more graphic, and brutal, magazines that you hadn't even known existed—taped to the walls, and on your locker. When a photo of two humping monkeys appeared in the lunchroom, with *NAT* scrawled above the submissive monkey's head, instead of throwing it in the bin you noted the location and date on the back, and kept it.

You recorded everything after that. Every piece of demeaning graffiti filed or photographed with the camera kept in your locker. The first time you tried to lodge a complaint, you took with you the crudely-drawn image of a naked female with tiny boobs and an exaggerated quaff hairstyle, on her back, knees spread and Foo peering out from the lip of the cavernous vagina. The shift supervisor's response was, 'You need to learn to take a joke, Luv. Anyway, there's no way to prove that drawing is meant to be you.'

You hadn't come out at work, knowing the additional shit you'd cop if the men had another prejudice to play with. But that hot summer night at the Carrington, instantly smitten by Belle, you'd thrown caution to the wind.

It was almost funny how Groper's face changed, once he'd worked out what he was watching.

Nige would never have let on, maybe Groper didn't either. There were other BHP men in that bar. Either way, word spread fast. Invitations to threesomes and loud discussions of how lezzos 'did it' were soon another manifestation of workplace 'bonhomie'.

Your first big mistake was not telling Sparkie you didn't want his recommendation for the apprenticeship award. The second was Belle.

You shift uncomfortably. Sitting for long in one position is always a problem.

Across the river not much has changed. It is hard to imagine that immense space empty, the only sounds the flap and moan of old corrugated iron, punctuated by the crackle of sparks from the angle grinders.

A dull roar rolls across the water. An excavator moves slowly backwards to tension the cables. The wind slaps cold against your face as you crank the car window right down.

Cold against your face was the first sensation you felt when you regained consciousness on the concrete floor of the steelmaking shed. Followed by pain everywhere except in your legs. Doped up in the back of the ambulance, you'd pleaded groggily with the Ambo beside you to promise your back wasn't broken. What could he say except wait, and hope?

It wasn't broken. But maybe you didn't hope hard enough, because the shattered vertebrae couldn't mend straight, and the nerve damage has lasted.

Your father was more shocked than anyone about the court case, saying, 'Don't do it, Natasha. Those men were your mates.' He never came to the proceedings. Nige was your main support, even though it was clear he would end up damned by association.

Not long after the court ruling, Nige left his job and went back to Forster. Said he'd had enough.

The roaring intensifies. Across the river, the vast shed shudders. Slowly, it starts to lean. You once saw an elephant shot, on TV. The shock as doom cracked, and life moved to non-life. The enormous beast swayed as everything that held it in place siphoned away, then folded in on itself, solidity crumpling. The high metal walls of the steelmaking shed collapse with the same inconceivability. Percussion, more than sound, fills your chest and the echoing cavity of your head.

History rises in decades of coaldust and rust, flakes of exploitable minerals and workers, the skeletal parts of birds, possums, rats, cockroaches and spiders, the detritus caked on every rafter and door lintel or lodged in the footprint of every dismantled machine, billowing into the sky.

You pull that sight deep into your lungs.

The black plume hangs for a moment, Vesuvius erupting, Hiroshima annihilated, before the wind takes it, smearing that grit and stench and pain above the city like a flag. A salute to the workers and long-suffering downwind residents of Stockton, Mayfield and Carrington. A pall that says more about Newcastle's subjugation to BHP, than any monument the company could build in steel.

Power registered intermittently through a circuit in the steelmaking shed. Needle directed you to climb the ladder to check the junction box, saying he'd ensure the circuit stayed off in the switchboard.

There was decay in your nostrils, the stench of something dead. A putrescent rat body jammed beneath the junction box. Gagging, you prepared to remove it.

You remember the flash, as your screwdriver met the connector.

Needle, the prick. Who had sidled up to you after the apprenticeship awards and hissed, 'Suckarse'. Who was stupid enough to laugh to men in the lunchroom, including Nige, about how a dead rat could end up lodged under a junction-box. Who blustered in the witness box, 'A bit of a joke. We all have to hack it. Just part of the job.' And whose testimony was stupid enough in court to reasonably doubt. As Maggie Olsen quickly made evident.

It wasn't the rat, or the height. The power circuit was still live. Recoil threw you off the ladder.

'Just a joke,' 'Man up,' 'Part of the job.' Phrases repeated over and over during the long weeks of the court case. You didn't expect to win, but Maggie worked through every word recorded in your notebooks, and called almost every man listed to the stand.

There was no hint of humour as Needle watched you put on your dust mask and gloves. He put that rat there. He sent you up that ladder.

Silence. You glance toward the F100. The men in its tray sit slumped, as if the wind has been knocked out of them.

Like the punch to your guts when Belle said she was over it all—your rehab, the courtroom.

Doors slam. The F100 revs, and is gone. You listen to the other cars leaving.

One figure remains, still in his folding chair, staring across the river. Sparkie, the loyal company man. He must have been hit for six in 1997, when BHP announced it was pulling out of Newcastle. Wham. No more work until retirement, no collective bargaining, thousands to compete with in the search for other jobs. Workers, community, the city itself, sold down the river.

'In for a penny, in for a pound,' Bert used to say whenever there was a whiff of industrial action. So, after long months of dragging yourself through rehab, you'd thought, Why not?

Maggie Olsen was a local solicitor who was determined to effect cultural change at the Works. 'Don't limit this to a compensation claim, Natasha,' she'd said. 'It should be an industrial grievance. That's your job now, to stand up for future women in the workplace, so they don't have to face the shit you've been through.'

Maggie was elated by the win. She said it was a landmark decision, and your lists and notebooks won the day.

You felt like a husk.

Bert came along to the courtroom several times for support, and tried to encourage other union members to go along. The day he came to tell you he wouldn't need to come back, he'd shaken your hand, saying, 'You were a damn good apprentice, Natasha. I can't say I'm happy about all this, but I admire your gumption.'

You'd sobbed as you watched him walk away.

You reverse the Cami and start following the wheel tracks through the flattened weeds.

Bert doesn't turn as you pass.
Your back hurts like hell.

06: 2007 Killer

Chi finally gets his mum to relent about having to complete Year 12.

'Okay,' Mai says. 'But school starts back in a week. If you haven't found a job by then, I'll change my mind. So, you'd better think fast about what you want to do.'

She's more cut and dried since she set up her own psychology clinic.

'Something outside,' Chi says. 'Working with my hands, instead of my stupid brain.'

'The only stupid thing about your brain, is it lets you call yourself stupid.'

The next day she hands him a Garden Kingdom advert.

'It's a good thing you got your P plates before Christmas, because the job's out at Sandgate, and requires a driving licence.'

Chi reads the boss's name, and goes cold. There wouldn't be many Marjanović́s in Newcastle. It has to be Danny's family.

Danny was still called Bogdan, when he turned up in high school. He was two years older than the rest of Chi's year. His family migrated from Croatia, so he didn't speak much English. He didn't need to. He pinched or twisted arms if he wanted someone's lunch, or seat, or place in a team. When he worked out why kids laughed when they called him 'Bog' or 'Bogger,' he changed his name to Danny. Calling him anything else led to fights he always won.

Chi never had to fight Danny, but he copped plenty of casual punches. One day Mishell Mathers, Chi's best mate since kindy, stepped between the two of them and told Danny, 'Punch me instead.' Fist raised, Danny looked like he was going to do it, but Mishell stared him down and Danny walked away without a word.

After that Danny left Chi alone, but Mish would call out, 'Hey, Danny' when she saw him, so he'd acknowledge her. She was the one who noticed when Danny came to school with bruises.

'Not this job,' Chi tells his mum. 'I'll find something else.'

'Call them,' she says.

Chi's mum lets him take her car out to Sandgate, so he brings Shanti along for the ride. He'd take her everywhere, if he could. His sister Cass had handed him the pup for his fifteenth birthday, a licky nine-week-old bundle of caramel and cream fluff. Shanti's darker now, a proper red Border Collie. She's super intelligent and easy to train, but still crazy energetic, even though she's nearly three.

Garden Kingdom is in a factory area with no shade. Chi drives in slowly, checking out the different bays and equipment. He sees a couple of guys talking outside the machinery shed, but there seems to be no-one else around. Parking near the raised container with the sign, 'Site Office', he winds the car windows down and tells Shanti to stay. Climbing the half-flight of metal steps to the office, he hopes the interview will be short.

He knocks beside the open door.

A deep voice bellows, 'Is there a bloody sign to knock? Walk in.'

The boss looks totally related to Danny. He has the same thickset build and wiry dark hair, but his accent is much stronger, Chi finds, when he says, 'Hello, Mr Marjanović.

'Good on Marjanović, but just call me Darko.' He looks Chi up and down.

'What are you, mate. A stick? I need someone with muscles. Ya gotta work all day in this place.'

Shanti chooses that moment to start barking.

'What's that? You gotta dog here?' Darko is already heading for the door. 'You don't leave a bloody dog stuck in a car in this heat.'

Chi follows him down the steps, feeling like he's just picked up a Get Out of Jail Free card in Monopoly.

Shanti is fine. By the time Darko is done with patting her, he knows Chi can handle a mower, and he thinks the wage sounds okay.

'Okay. That's good. Be here at 6.30 tomorrow morning and bring a bloody hat.'

That night, when his mum gets home from work, Chi tells her it's Shanti's fault he got the job.

At least one of them is happy.

At the top of the work schedule whiteboard, someone has laboriously taped *GARDEN KINGDOM LANDSCAP*, in yellow and green block letters.

Darko cleans the last worker's name from the top of the mowing column and writes Chi in its place. Chi reads. *Watt Moocher st mayfeld fr/Bk gar*, at the start of his list, and thinks of the science teacher he'd liked in Year 8 at high school, who left suddenly before the end of the year. It'd be weird, he thinks, if it's *that* Mr Watt.

He asks Darko for the street number and checks the UBD map. The house is on Moolcha Street, backing on to Throsby Creek. Chi pictures gardens spilling through back fences, a stream sneaking like a secret beneath overhanging branches.

The house is one of those little weatherboard and asbestos places that butt right onto the footpath, so there's only a narrow nature strip to worry about at the front. On his third visit, as he shoves grass clippings from the strip into a garbage bag, Chi decides the old man is off the planet. Doesn't give a shit about what I do out here, but as soon as I push the mower down the side path, he's out like a rocket. Squeaky wheels must be music to his ears.

Bk gar, he thinks. Calling Mr Watt's backyard a 'garden', is a serious stretch. There's a concrete path from the side of the house to the back steps, and another leading to the Hill's Hoist that sits dead centre in the big square of grass that Chi mows every fortnight. Beyond it, Throsby Creek is a wide concrete drain full of green slime and rubbish with only weeds and a few spindly eucalypts growing along the banks. Paling fences block the sight of it from most of the adjoining houses, but Mr Watt's place has a high cyclone-wire back fence with a padlocked gate. It feels like a prison. A solitary shrub grows in one corner of the yard: an old rosemary bush that might stand a chance if it had a good prune. Chi offered, but Mr Watt growled, 'Leave it.'

Each time Chi arrives around the back, Mr Watt is out there on his verandah, hunched in his scabby old armchair, head jutting like a goanna. Watching.

Normally, when you mow, you start at one end of a lawn and mow to the other, clean up, and leave. But the first time Chi came, the old man gave him a ruled-up drawing. Lines and arrows that started at the hoist, moved outwards in squares that crossed the centre path, and finished along the side path. Chi quickly learnt that the mower lines had to finish where each square started, and the machine manoeuvred onto the next track without leaving a cut-mark. But there is the blip of the rosemary bush. He has to mow a half square around it, which wrecks the whole pattern. Seriously weird, especially as the old man supervises every move, shouting 'Keep straight' or 'Wrong direction'. Also, not a blade of grass can be left behind. Even the last-minute gum leaves that blow from the trees across the drain have to be bagged and taken away.

Obsessed, Chi thinks as he starts the last careful lap of the lawn. And he never says thanks. What a shitty way to live. Nothing better to do than watch me mow, and only a drain to look out on. And there's never been any sign that he remembers me.

It is actually hard to believe Mr Watt *was* his Year 9 teacher. How could someone change so much? Sure, he was already pretty old back then, and other kids dissed his comb-track hair and old-man clothes, and the time he took to explain everything. But Chi liked him and his slow teaching. He remembers Mr Watt saying that patterns made things predictable, and if you understood a pattern, you could change it. Which sort of explains why Chi had done okay in science, maths and music. Because of the patterns. All the other subjects he'd been crap at.

It was in Mr Watt's science class that things at school took a nosedive. Chi grew to over six feet in Year 11, but back in Year 9 he was still a weed. He was sitting at a lab bench with Mish when Danny brought his stool over and plonked down on her other side. Mr Watt was at the board talking about electrical energy, drawing diagrams to show how a Walkman and a toaster drew power. When he wrote up *Kilowatt hour (kWh)* Danny nudged Mish and whispered. She grinned, raised her hand and called, 'Sir?'

Mr Watt had looked around smiling. All the teachers liked Mishell. She was a little bit cheeky, but she asked good questions. She said, '*Killerwatt*, Sir? Is that why people call you Killer?'

Everyone laughed, except Mr Watt. His smile stayed, but he looked sad at the same time.

'Very funny, Mishell,' he said. 'You're not the first person to ask me that and you won't be the last,' and he turned back to the board.

Chi could tell Mish felt uncomfortable. He asked in a whisper, 'Killer? Where did that come from?'

She rolled her eyes and said, 'Everyone calls him that.'

Leaning around her, Danny had said so everyone could hear, 'Yeah, fucktard *chink*, doncha know nothing?'

The rest of the class cracked up, and everyone started calling him Chink. Except Mish. But she started to hang out with Danny's gang and pretty much forgot he existed.

Not long after that lesson on energy, another teacher took over the science class and the School Principal announced at assembly that Mr Watt had retired. A few months later, Chi was walking Shanti with Mum in Islington Park, near where Throsby Creek escapes from the concrete canal and bikes and shopping trollies rust under the mangroves, when he saw Mr Watt ahead on the bridge. Chi gave a stupid shoulder-high girl wave, and Mr Watt waved back. Shanti reached him first. She lifted her paw and he bent down and shook it. Mr Watt looked a lot greyer. He introduced himself to Chi's mum and said, 'Your boy was the most enjoyable sort of pupil, because he thought things through.' Chi's mum was pleased. Mr Watt was the only teacher who ever said something good like that.

On the way home, Mai said, 'He's a nice man. It must be tough to keep going after such a tragedy in your life.'

'What tragedy?'

'I did tell you, but these days I never know when you're listening. A car accident. His daughter and both his grandchildren died. Mr Watt was driving. There were a lot of rumours about why the accident happened, but the coroner's report said he lost control because something broke in the car. An axle, I think. There was nothing he could do.'

Chi checks out Mr Watt's place as he loads up the work truck. The brown paint on the weatherboards is faded and there's black on their ridges and the sills, but most old houses in Mayfield have layers of that muck, even though the Steelworks closed a few years back. The place looks tidy, no cobwebs or junk lying about. The old man's like that, too. His clothes are old but he makes himself neat. His hair is white now and so thin you can see pink skin in the comb tracks.

Moolcha Street's dozy quiet is shattered by a woman yelling in the house three doors down. Squawking lorikeets erupt from the garden like a rainbow and fragment against the blue sky. Last time he was here, Chi had gone to check out that house's garden, after noticing from Mr Watt's back fence the laden mango and olive trees planted on the reserve, and pumpkin vines spilling out the gate. The front was chockers with fruit and nut trees, beds full of tomatoes, artichokes, basil, lettuce, and melons. Climbing back into the truck, he'd thought, so much food growing on that one little block. I want to have a place like that one day.

Back at the Kingdom, Chi walks into the office to find his boss slumped over his messy desk, staring at the computer. Normally he reefs his chair around on its castors and shouts 'Slowdown, ya dickhead' as soon as he hears Chi thunder up the metal steps, but his palms are pressed so tight to his ears that the rims would have to imprint. On the computer screen, a video pans over what looks like human bodies in a pit.

Chi taps Darko's shoulder. Darko lurches like he's been jabbed by an electric prod. He presses a back-key and the screen image changes.

'Darko? Are you okay?'

'Yeah.' Darko doesn't move.

'Darko?

'Shuddup.'

Darko brushes a work-stained hand though his wiry salt-and-pepper hair and pushes his chair back. He is a short, heavily-built man. The castors turn slowly.

'It's nothing,' he says flatly. No eye contact.

Chi hovers.

'*Shit* man. A headache, that's all.'

Chi looks helplessly around the office. 'Do you want, like, water or something?'

'*Nothing*. Forget it.'

Darko jabs his thumb at a plastic chair by the wall. 'Siddown. Talk me through these damn receipts of yours. They make no sense. You do this to me every time.'

A car horn blasts. Darko groans, prises himself from the chair and peers through the nicotine-stained nylon curtains.

'Sonofabitch. Not that whinging fuckin prick again. Just wait, will ya?'

Darko's bad temper is short-lived and his volatile moods no longer faze Chi. Leaning back in the plastic chair he stretches out his legs. The office is a mess. Boxes that should be in the storage container, full of gloves, cleats, super-size garbage bags, and trimmer chord, are half-unpacked. Food cartons and spilled folders spread over the desk and onto the floor.

The shouting outside continues.

Chi gathers the papers, taps them straight, and puts them in piles beside Darko's keyboard. The headline on the screen reads *Milošević dead before trial end*. The man in the photo could be anybody's uncle. Broad face, dark button eyes, hair receding in puffy tufts. He looks a bit like a koala. Chi scans the page. Places he's never heard of, except for one. Croatia. He is trying to make more sense of the report when he hears Darko bellow his name, telling tell him to get the fuck back to work.

Mostly there's no-one home when Chi arrives to mow, the clients at work or escaping somewhere from the noise. The retired women in Tighes Hill zip out their front gate as he unloads his gear, calling 'Off to the gym again.' Darko reckons that when he started the business, heaps of ladies invited him in. For 'refreshments', he says, waggling his eyebrows. Chi has never been invited in. The best he's managed was a glass of water one hot day when the Tighes Hill women came home from gym early. They don't seem the type to invite a tradesman in, though. Tradeswomen maybe.

Sometimes, if the owners aren't there, he mows a pattern in the grass before he gets down to business. Or his graffiti tag. He's been practicing the Chan Buddhist circle, a perfect, almost-closed O. He found lots of the circles painted on heavy paper in an old box of his grandfather's, that his mum gave him, and looked up what they were. There were photos of his grandfather too, with his family in China. 'You look like him,' Mai said, but Chi thinks his grandfather's eyes look way narrower. He likes that the Chan circle is a symbol for something that's empty and full at the same time. It's also a secret C, for Chi, which means 'life force' in Chinese. That's what he calls himself now, having found a way to subvert his hated nickname from school. And nobody's going to guess the Chan circle is his tag.

Garden Kingdom clients don't care what you do with their garden, as long as the work is neat and done on time. Nobody watches, except the old man, though he shouts less these days. Slumped in his chair like a collapsed mummy, he could be asleep.

Magpies squawk in the eucalypts beyond Throsby Creek's scummy trickle. The day is hot and Chi is keen to get on to the Tighes Hill job, where the garden is shady. Words start to swirl in his head:

all I get for mow-in
is this old badass moan-in
under his breath,
waitin' for death

Maybe he'll find a wall to paint it up, green letters on a purple background, the edges shredding like flying grass clippings.

Without thinking, he swings the mower in a circle.

The shouts come through the earmuffs.

Mr Watt is on the edge of his chair. His arms jerk like a string puppet, and spit flies from his mouth.

Chi cuts the mower and reefs off the muffs. They stare at each other in the cut-grass silence. The old man raises his arm and wipes his mouth on the long sleeve of his blue checked shirt. He gazes at the damp patch.

Chi calls, 'Sorry!'

Mr Watt looks back. The angry furrows on his face replaced by a different expression. He cranks himself up from the chair and shambles towards his backdoor and into the house.

Chi pulls on the muffs, restarts the mower and begins again from the clothesline. It was bad enough, being caught out stuffing around, but that look on the old man's face was way worse. Like I've made him ashamed, he thinks.

Even the drone of the mower can't shift that word from his head.

After work, Chi grabs Shanti's Frisbee and lead and takes her across the road from his house to Wickham Park. He throws the Frisbee high. Shanti leaps vertically, like a bloke ballet dancer, her long hair rippling. Her jaws snap. Perfect catch.

Chi can't stop thinking about Mr Watt. Darko charges by the hour including fifteen minutes for travel. The Moolcha Street job is straightforward, ten minutes to mow and clean up out front, twenty-five max in the back including edge-trimming, raking and bagging, so usually he gets away early. Today he stayed the full forty-five, looking for more grass and leaves to sweep up. Like an apology.

The old man hadn't come back out.

Shanti pulls up, puffed. They head home, skirting the old bowling club in the corner of the park. There's a weedy green at one end that could be perfect for a community garden. Chi leans on the fence and stares at the sign on the front of the building. CROATIAN WICKHAM SPORTS CLUB. The Croat has been part of his childhood landscape, but he's never wondered about its name. He thinks of the bodies he saw on Darko's computer.

At dinner, he asks his mum what she knows about Croatia and the war. She sighs.

'Not much. Except that nationalism and religion are a bad mix, and the human race isn't nearly as civilised as we like to believe. Use my computer if you want to find out more.'

Chi starts with Wikipedia and follows links. He ends up with images of the Srebrenica massacre. In bed, he dreams he is on a path in a forest, foraging for mushrooms. All he can find are weird red fungi that look like starfish and stink like rotting meat. He hears voices. They are coming from the fungi. An eyeless grey face calls to him in a language he doesn't understand.

Darko smacks his head with his palm, swings his chair around from the Football Federation Australia Cup fixtures chart on his computer screen to glare at Chi, and explodes.

'Why do the idiot donkeys want to fuck with NSW Soccer and change the name to NSW Football so it sounds like what those fuckin Victorian pansies play?'

Chi expected to be yelled at, but not about football.

Darko's dark eyes take on a yellow gleam. 'Fuck, you're a useless prick.'

Chi stares back. He works hard, and Darko knows it, and the Kingdom is always losing workers. Two days ago, Chi heard another useless prick tell the boss to shove his job where the sun never shines.

Darko pulls in a long breath. 'Killer rang last night. How hard can it be to mow an old fart's backyard straight?'

'Killer?' It's a shock to hear that name from Darko.

'Old man Watt. Taught you at school, yeah? Same as my kid brother, Bogdan?'

The phone shrills. Darko picks it up and gestures for Chi to stay.

Chi wanders to the window, pushes the sticky curtains apart, and watches one of the loader drivers take a load of bush-rock towards the new storage bays. The loader bucket tilts. Rocks thud to the ground like bad memories.

He frowns. Why would Danny even bother telling his brother Mr Watt's school nickname? Darko hardly ever bothers with people's real names. Like, he always refers to the worker at the yard who is openly gay as The Pansy. Now Mr Watt will always be Killer, and Darko will smirk like he invented the joke.

Which makes what happened, the first time Chi saw Danny at the Kingdom, so weird.

On that day, he'd been heading to the office, he'd seen Darko abusing someone loudly at the bottom of the steps. Someone who looked a lot like Darko, but bigger. Chi had turned away, but too late. He heard Danny call, with what sounded like relief, 'Hey, that's Chink. He works here? Get over here and say gidday, Chink.'

Chi looked back to see Darko cuff Danny over the head.

'Bogdan? What'd you call him? His fuckin' name's Chi. Don't you forget it.' Looking over to Chi, Darko yelled, 'If this prick kid brother of mine gives you trouble, you tell me and I'll sort him.'

Danny shuffled his feet and looked at the ground.

After that, it was like there'd been a sort of no-man's zone between Danny and Chi when they ran into each other. Nothing bad, though. They'd say gidday, but keep their distance. Danny generally only appears at the Kingdom if there's a worker short, and when he's there Darko yells more than usual. The way Danny cops it, not answering back, reminds Chi of how he'd coped with Danny at school.

Darko's argument over the phone is getting louder. The hardest thing about Darko, Chi decides, is never being sure what he means. It sometimes feels like there's something black inside his boss, for him to scare his brother like that. He thinks guiltily of Mish being upset when Danny had bruises. For Chi, that was a sign of something being right in the world—Danny copping what he doled out. Maybe Darko had been Chi's secret benefactor. He does say weird stuff when he's pissed off, though. Like, one time, telling a slow-paying client that he needed his head shot off. And another day, in the office, he'd slammed the phone down, saying, 'I want to snap that bastard's neck like a rabbit,' and when Chi laughed, because it seemed a jokey image, Darko fixed him with a death stare and said, 'What? You think I couldn't kill a man?'

It's hard to tell with Darko. Probably all talk.

Darko drops the phone on his desk and, barely taking a breath, he says, 'I'm telling you, Chi, it's a fuck-off when clients complain to me about idiots I pay. Pull that trick again on Killer, you'll be fired.'

'Sorry. I won't. I didn't mean to get Mr Watt riled.'

And that was that. Back to normal.

A couple of weekends later, Mai drives Chi and Shanti up to Cass's place at Dungog. Chi and his sister tear around the bush tracks on the quads, with Shanti chasing after. At home on Sunday night, Shanti isn't her usual bouncy self, but Chi puts it down to all the exercise.

Early the next morning, his mum drives off for a five-day conference in Coff's Harbour. Chi, about to catch the bus to work, notices Shanti wobble in her back legs. He finds the tick and feels sick about not checking her over the night before. There's no way to get her to the vet. He calls the Kingdom. And is blown away when Darko says, 'You gotta look after your dog, mate. Get in here. You can take her to the vet in the truck.'

When Chi gets back to the Kingdom, Darko asks, 'What'd the vet say?'

'Touch and go,' Chi says, his throat tight. 'She has to stay overnight.'

'Your mum's away all week? So, take the bloody truck home. Either way, tomorrow you're gonna need to pick her up. If she's okay, bring her here.'

The thought of 'either way' makes Chi feel like crying.

Shanti still can't walk when he picks her up from the vet the next morning. He parks the truck at work and Darko comes over from the office. Seeing Shanti on the passenger seat, he opens the door, leans in and puts his face against her neck. He looks a bit emotional when he stands up.

'Still not great, eh? So, keep the truck till your mum gets back. Bring her to work till she's stronger.'

The weather is cool when Chi returns to Moolcha Street. Shanti has spent the last couple of days in the Kingdom office, but he decides she'll be fine in the truck. He leaves the passenger window rolled down and a bowl of water on the floor.

Halfway around the back lawn, he flicks a glance at Mr Watt. Shanti is on the verandah beside him, and he is slowly stroking her head. Something about how they look tells Chi it is okay to leave her there.

After he finishes the clean-up, Mr Watt beckons with his hand. Chi walks up the verandah steps. The old man has to tilt sideways in his vinyl chair to look up. His grey cardigan looks like it should be on a bigger man, and the wrinkles beside his mouth are wet.

Chi says, 'You used to be my teacher, at school. I was sorry when you left, and I'm sorry I mucked around with your lawn last time I was here.'

Mr Watt stares up with milky eyes. 'I know who you are. Why aren't you at school, finishing your HSC?'

Chi shuffles his feet and looks at the floor. 'School sucked.'

Mr Watt's face furrows into the encouraging smile that Chi remembers. 'Don't let that school dictate the pattern of your life. Go to TAFE if you like working outdoors. Get a certificate in horticulture, tree lopping, or landscape design. Build up your own business.'

He gives Shanti a pat. 'Next time, bring her too.'

It isn't so easy to take Shanti back a fortnight later. Chi's mum is away again and there's no point asking Darko, who's totally pissed over another worker leaving.

Chi sneaks home to Wickham with the truck, to pick Shanti up. He'll drop her home after Mr Watt's.

Shanti, back to her old self, leads the way up the side path, pampas tail waving. She heads straight for the verandah. Mr Watt isn't in his chair.

Chi worries as he mows. Mr Watt has never missed a day and he didn't look great last time. Maybe he's in hospital.

Job done. he calls Shanti. She is at the back door, whining. Chi's skin prickles.

The door isn't locked. Mr Watt has fallen face-down across the lounge in the living room. His arm hangs over the side. His hand is blue. Shanti licks it and settles down beside him.

Chi calls an ambulance and wanders around the room. Photos line the shelves. Most of them feature a youngish woman and two little kids. The kids are playing in a sandpit, or on a swing, or running through a shady garden. There are glimpses of Throsby Creek through the shrubs along the back fence, and the one at the far end looks like a vigorous rosemary bush.

House prices in Mayfield have shot up, since the Steelworks closed, and places sell quickly. It's late autumn when Chi drives the truck back into the Kingdom and reefs on the handbrake. He has five minutes to get to the bus.

'Chi, get in here,' Darko yells through the office window. 'There's an extra job on your list tomorrow.'

Darko's usual slow turn of the office chair as Chi walks in the door no longer seems ominous.

'Gotta do a clean-up on Killer's place. Real estate wants photos.'

Chi stares down at his boss, and says slowly, 'Mr Watt's place.'

Darko stares back. 'Yeah. Right. Mr Watt.'

'I'll need two hours, if nothing's been done for the last couple of months.'

Darko laughs. 'What, you reckon I'm stupid? I'm charging out at four.'

There are cobwebs around Mr Watt's front windows. Chi peers through at the empty rooms. When he finishes the nature strip, he grabs a couple of extra tools and rolls the mower down the side path, listening to the squeak the wheels make.

He uses the loppers to remove the dead wood and collapsed branches from the rosemary bush, trims it into shape with the secateurs, and takes a few cuttings to strike at home. He stands back to check out his work. It will grow lush and upright if the place isn't levelled by developers.

He considers the lawn. Mowing standard parallel strips for the agent's photos doesn't feel right. Darko probably never knew about the squares and probably wouldn't care, the clients get what they ask for. But Chi hopes that whatever made Mr Watt choose that pattern to look out on, it might have given him some sort of peace. Chi's mum had suggested going to his funeral, but there was nothing in the paper. Maybe there wasn't even a funeral. Maybe no words were said.

It's only grass, Chi thinks. If I screw up, I can come back in my own time to fix it.

The grass is rank. He sets the blades higher than normal, so it won't look too patchy. Mowing, he mulls over what Mr Watt said about making his own pattern.

When he's done, Chi checks his work from the verandah. Concentric squares, exactly as Mr Watt wanted them.

He thinks of his grandfather's calligraphy circles. So many different versions of the same thing, stored in an old box. Like a shape to live your life by.

Chi looks over Mr Watt's lawn and visualises eight points equally distant from the base of the clothesline. Committing them to memory, he returns to the mower, sets the blades low, and re-starts the motor.

Slowly, and with full attention, he mows a perfect, nearly closed, Chan circle.

07: 2007 Dupain

By the time Matt pulls up on the crest beside Newcastle Beach Surf Club, he is panting. The light is flat, and everything looks monochrome: the steely sea and towering grey clouds, the sullen coal ship, *Pasha Bulker*, beached in the shallows below Nobbys lighthouse, even the people jostling at the sea-wall rail for a better view.

Disappointed, he zips his jacket against the cold wind and tells himself, Work with it. Like Max Dupain. Fix up the contrasts in the developing bath.

Suddenly the scene becomes vivid, as though someone's flicked a bank of floodlights on. The sea seethes with every tone of green, the ship's white superstructure gleams against purple and violet clouds, its hull blazes blood red. Matt swings around, looking for the light source. Beyond the choppy river and wharves and silos of Carrington, sunlight streams through a low slit in the clouds.

But too low. Nearly sunset.

Urgently, he shrugs off his backpack and pulls out the Pentax, hoping the magic will last. What an idiot, leaving it this late. He should have guessed finding a car park would be hopeless. Days and days of insane storms and flooding, and now Newcastle has cabin-fever. Everyone wants to be outside, and they want to be here, watching the drama they've seen unfold on TV happen in real time. He checks the camera settings, annoyed he still has to think it through, and fires off a dozen shots.

The brightness flicks off. Everything leaden again. The magic moment gone.

Matt lowers the camera. That's when the immensity in front of him hits: the *Pasha Bulker*'s vastness, her domination of beach, sea and sky. Waves pound her hull. They surge up high above her deck, and fall back in cataracts of foam. One completely engulfs her bridge in an explosion of white, and the crowd screams its approval, goading the sea on, wanting to see it crush, annihilate. It could be a footy grand-final, or gladiators battling.

Every second person wields a camera. Happy snaps will flood Facebook, be sent to the press. Matt is failing in his TAFE photography course so far, but this assignment, to capture the essence of his city, sounded easy. But he's just about blown it, wandering for too long around the port and industrial precincts imagining how good his shots would be. Four days ago he was in the TAFE darkroom lifting his images from the developing tray, and seeing that each one was a dud. Coal loaders, ships, and machinery, shot from different angles but no balance, no killer effects of light and shadow, nothing that could drag his grades out of the hole they're in. That's when he heard, on the darkroom radio, that a storm had hit Newcastle. Over next couple of hours, the updates on the ABC started to get serious. Reports of flooding in the city centre and winds and currents driving a giant ship towards Nobbys Beach, more and more roads being affected. When he heard of impending road closures that could affect his route back to New Lambton, where he shared a flat with a couple of other students, he'd left his photos pegged, done a quick clean up, and bolted for home.

There was no way that he'd expected to be stuck at home for three days: the city assailed by ferocious winds and rain and gridlocked by water: the river and creeks and canals backed up by king tides, so that flooding had nowhere to go but into the underground carparks and over sports fields and swimming pools, into every house in the inner suburbs that wasn't on higher ground.

When he'd heard on the radio that the roads leading to the waterfront had finally re-opened, he'd jumped straight into his car. The coal ship still being stranded seemed like a gift. Driving through Hamilton, he'd passed street after street where sodden carpets and furniture were piled outside front fences, and cars had mudlines to their windows, but there was no time to stop to look or to help. Instead, he'd focused on ways to change his teacher's opinion that he's a slack-arse, planning the cool upward angles he'd be able to shoot from the beach. The stricken ship's prow with the giant storm clouds above, that soaring perspective Max Dupain used to make his industrial images so overpowering—although Matt would take his images further, capture the shock of something mighty being crippled.

But now that he's here, he sees blue and white police tape cordoning off the entire beach and dune above it. There's no way he can get down to the ship. Like the captain of *Pasha Bulker*, he's left his move too late.

Dismally, Matt re-evaluates the grey scene. Maybe he can work with the grungy light, but he needs an edge, something beyond the predictable. A downwards perspective could maybe accentuate the stranded ship's helplessness against the voracious elements? But where to go for elevation? He looks for a better vantage point. The beach pavilion is too low. Fort Scratchley is higher, but further away and he can see the lookout already has a mob clustered there. He looks up at the balcony of the old Lifeguard's building beside him. It too is packed with onlookers, but he'll surely be able to find a spot? He dodges down through the knots of people crowding the broad concrete steps. Reaching the door, he finds a rugged-looking bloke blocking him.

'Yeah mate, you and a million others.'

Matt swears as a kid bumps him. He gazes back up the steps. So many milling people, so many different expressions. He raises the camera. Uses the viewfinder to scan for possible subjects. Swings back to a flare of white hair.

The old woman is hunched against the brick wall of the building, her hands jammed between her trackie-clad knees. Her jacket billows, the cold wind merciless. She is still, while everyone else seems mobile, elbowing for a place at the handrail or bracing against the wind as they scurry about, all intent on the beached coal carrier.

Not as intent as she is.

She is about fifteen metres away, and passing bodies interrupt Matt's view, but he stays where he is, out of her sightline. He carefully turns the lens to sharpen the focus. The colours are good, dark pants and rust-coloured jacket against the cream paint of the building. In close-up her hair is shoulder-length and yellow-white, her profile dominated by a beaky nose. Hawkish, he thinks. The next moment, as a gust of wind riffles her hair like feathers and wobbles the sagging skin under her chin, he decides *chookish* is a better description. His gran used to keep Isa Brown chickens in the backyard of her fibro at Stockton. This old dame looks like one of them. Even her jacket is brown.

'That's it, Chookie, stay right there.'

His finger presses slowly. Click. The shutter closing like the blink of a chook's eye. Again. A third time.

It is hard to hold the camera steady. Looking for something to brace against, he moves to a metal light post. Steadies. Raises the camera again. Curious faces turn his way.

A knot of teenagers barges past: torn denims, scuffed skate shoes, the swish of nylon parkas. A girl shrieks, 'What's he doin'? Not even photographin' the fucken boat. Watta dickhead!'

Bogans, Matt thinks, but he accepts that he's part of their day's entertainment. Everyone's here for the spectacle and anything different is game. Their hoots of laughter wash over him as he re-centres the old woman in his lens. He manages another dozen shots before her head starts to turn. He lowers the camera and swings away, sure that she won't have seen him. He's got enough, and anyway she's not what he came for.

He looks back at the ship. The light has changed again. The industrial greys that accentuated its vulnerability have gone. Everything is lit by the last of the sun, clouds pink and blue, Nobbys headland and its white lighthouse edged with cartoonish gold. The *Pasha Bulker* looks smaller, its hull like red plastic. A ship in an old movie poster.

Pissed off, and wishing he hadn't wasted time on the old chook, Matt weaves his way to where people hang like clots of weed along the wooden handrail. He finds a space and squeezes in. The elderly couple to his right tutt and move sideways. Two squealing girls to his left are doing a *Titanic*, one clutching the other who leans, arms outstretched, over the rail. Their blonde-streaked hair streams behind them. They laugh as he takes a shot of them with the ship in the background.

Below him, the breakers are the glassy green of old wine bottles. They crash, the wash surging right up the seawall. From here he can see how much the beach has been altered. Sand gouged away from the ship's near-side and dumped over the rocks beyond the prow. He thinks of the worried-looking engineer on last night's TV news saying *Pasha*'s outer hull was cracked and if the inner one failed there'd be a disastrous fuel spill. That's why it's still way too risky to try towing the ship to deeper waters.

What happens if they can't shift it, Matt wonders. What if it stays stranded and disintegrates for decades, like the wreck of the Sygna, up in the middle of nowhere, halfway along Stockton Beach? But this isn't the middle of nowhere, it's the middle of Newcastle. This humungous beast of a ship could change how people feel about this beach, and Nobbys, and the city, forever.

He pulls a cloth from his bag and is carefully cleaning the salt from his camera lens when the people around him roar. His head jerks up. A wave avalanche buries the deck and bridge. He swings the camera up, but too late. Deflated, he swears, and the oldies tutt again.

But an even bigger wave is coming. The blonde girls stop screaming and the crowd holds its collective breath. Half-squatting, Matt braces his elbow on the handrail. Wait, he tells himself. It's all about timing.

The wave hits the ship with an audible crack. It surges up and up, higher than the funnel, higher than the comms tower.

Matt clicks furiously through the shrieks of awe and approval. The ship's bulk seems to list beneath the weight of water. Through his feet he feels the shudder of the hull grinding into the beach. Everything is moving, the condensing air, swooping seagulls.

The wave that follows reaches barely halfway up the ship's side, and Matt joins the mutual sigh of disappointment. It's as if the days of deluge that they've all lived through—the city brought to its knees by the flooding and power-cuts, school children separated from their frantic parents, people waist-deep in their homes, the sick, elderly and birthing women unable to reach hospitals or other assistance, even the shock news of drownings—have not been enough. They want the waves bigger. They want the *Pasha Bulker* to keel onto its side, split in two, spill its disaster of fuel. Deliver a soap opera they can lose themselves in.

The clouds are moving out to sea. Matt extricates himself from the crowd and heads towards the Lighthouse. Maybe he'll find a better vantage point along the track.

Ahead, three middle-aged women laugh as they stagger in the

buffeting air. Behind him someone calls, 'Hey, Max, Max!'

A girl in a red plastic raincoat with the hood up swings in front of him. Brown eyes, wide mouth curving in a dolphin smile, top front teeth slightly crossed. Strands of long dark hair whip her face.

'Sorry? You mean me? I'm not ...'

She grins. 'Yeah, saw the camera and knew it was you. You're Max Dupain, right?'

Matt shrugs, non-committal.

'You remember? Over at the foreshore? That night you came and took the shots of us.' She laughs, 'You know, of us *Hoons*.'

He does know. Dusk, last summer. Hotted-up cars strung along Wharf Road. Rev-heads grooming their vehicles, stroking duco as if it were a woman's breast. Revving engines, power displays, donuts, clutch-drops, burnouts. Cop cars flashing blue and red. Matt had wandered down with his camera. Maybe he could take a few good shots, sell them to a magazine. But he hadn't counted on feeling so exposed, how confronting it would feel to point an obvious camera at someone likely to be hostile. After being told to fuck off more times than he could count, he gave up on the people shots and focused on the cars, occasionally graced by wannabee gangsters striking exaggerated poses, fingers flipping the bird. Hearing a deep voice shout, 'Hey fucktard! Get over here,' he had turned to discover that he was the object of the invitation. He'd walked nervously towards the half dozen young people, roughly his age who, showcased by a streetlight, lounged against two cars parked illegally on the grass verge. Matt was called wanker, shitbox, and names he could never have invented, but they'd let him shoot for fifteen minutes.

'I'm Shelly, remember?' the red-coat girl says.

Matt remembers. Of the two girls in that group, she was the dark skinny one, dwarfed by the bulk of the guy with his arm slung around her neck. The one who'd called him over. The one the others called Bull. It was clear he was boss of the pack, and of Shelly, but, Matt remembers, Bull hadn't called her Shelly, back then. He'd used another name.

'You said you'd send us those pix,' Shelly is saying, 'but you never did?'

Nose ring, eyes heavily outlined in black. Pretty. Challenging.

Matt thinks fast. 'That bit of paper you gave me? With the email? Lost it. Sorry.'

'Yeah?' She sounds sceptical. 'So I'll give you it again.'

Impulsively, Matt brings up his camera. Shelley laughs, moves into glamour poses. The backwards over-the-shoulder wink, the bent-kneed cutesy Japanese finger-on-cheek. She flings herself in a spin, the wind whips her raincoat open and the hood flies off. Head back, eyes closed, her laugh is wild, buoyant. Later, developing the shot, Matt would see the curve of her stomach and think, seventeen, maybe eighteen, already pregnant, and feel bad for being judgemental.

Gasping a little, Shelly digs in her raincoat pockets.

'No pen. You got one?'

Matt shakes his head.

'Then get this into your brain, Max Dupain,' she says fiercely. 'It's shelly eighty-nine at bigpond dot com. No caps, Shelly with one e. You gunna remember that?'

Matt stands at the highest point he can find. The sun has gone and the light's dimming fast. The best he can hope for is something gothic, the spooky potential for that mammoth hulk to destroy. From here it looks as though only a few metres of wave wash separate the ship from the beach. If he could get down there he could probably wade out and touch that rearing prow. How high from the bottom of the hull to the bridge, he wonders. Ten storeys? More? And some of the biggest waves sprayed twenty or thirty metres higher than the deck.

Wet-suited surfers, dwarfed by the bulk beside them, take advantage of the long break the ship has created. Matt has taken a few shots when something zooms across his viewfinder. A jet-skier, slewing around in the troughs, crazily close to the ship. Matt holds his breath, expecting disaster, the backflip as the ski guns up a crest, vehicle and driver flung into the air, the crash into the hull, but he lowers the camera. The light's shit for distance, and the cold's getting to him. No point wasting more film.

Walking back towards the surf club Matt wishes Shelly-with-one-e had forgotten his lie about being Max Dupain. Dupain's work has been the holy grail ever since Matt began to get serious about photography, those classic shots of fit young surf-lifesavers racing, or draped in brief swimmers around sea-baths, and his famous 'Sunbaker', a water-beaded young man lying on sand. Dupain used light and shadow to define a cheekbone, jawline, the hard muscles of a boy's thigh. Stillness, that's what he photographed. Stillness beyond something snared with a simple click of the shutter. A sense of his subjects caught out of time. When Dupain came to Newcastle a couple of decades back, he'd created a portrait of a city with his perspectives of industry and shipping and buildings that soared. As if he'd captured the weight of concrete and steel in the act of lifting up and away. Paused for that one, still moment.

That's what Matt had wanted to channel today, shooting the *Pasha Bulker*. He shrugs. Probably another fail, but the Shelly pics might turn out okay.

Shelly sea-shell, he thinks. *Conch.* That's what Shelly's boyfriend called her, and when he did, Matt remembers, she had flinched.

Driving back home to his gran's house in Stockton, that night after the hoons, he had speculated on what Bull had meant by that name. And what made Bull suss that I'm gay, he had wondered as well. I don't walk or talk or dress any differently from anyone else. I don't wear a sticky note with 'gay-boy' stuck to my forehead like in a game of Who Am I.

Matt had been living with this grandmother since he was thirteen, seven years, and she was already old back then. She was asleep when he got home, the door to her room half-open to her soft snores. Leaving the living room light off, he walked to the glass shelves beside the window that housed her collection of shells. When he picked up the big conch, he could feel the grate of the hairline crack that ran through its bell-curve. Gran called it a bailer shell, and it was precious to her because her dad had brought it home from his last stint as a seaman in the Pacific, not long before he died. Matt had loved that big old shell since he'd first been trusted to hold it, it's delicate brown and orange sand-patterns, the sea-whisper when he held it to his ear. There was a hole the size of a ten-cent piece carved in its side that you blew through.

It took him a long time to master that sweet, low stomach-gripping note. That was before he dropped it, when his gran was away on an old-people's bus trip. Matt had been body surfing on Stockton beach, and brought a friend home for some food. The boy had picked up the conch and slid his hand inside, 'Hey, look at this. Just like a cunt.' But Matt's eyes were on the boy's brown back. How his knobby spine curved in then out down to the little mound and then his bum-crack, just visible over his daggy board shorts. After the boy left, Matt had picked up the shell and run his fingers over the fleshy pucker where the shell opened. Picturing his friend's buttocks, he'd slid his hand in and, awkwardly clutching the shell, slipped the other hand into his shorts and jerked until the shell fell to the floorboards. He had returned the conch to its place on the shelf, but it never again produced that sweet deep note. Gran never mentioned it. Perhaps she didn't pick it up anymore.

Last year Matt came home one afternoon to find her crumpled and stiff by the window. She must have clutched the shelves as she'd fallen. Shells were scattered over the floor and the conch was in pieces.

Matt shivers, his wind jacket no longer warm enough. The streetlights are on and most of the crowd has gone. Lured by the cawing of seagulls, he returns to the rail above the seawall. The tide has gone out a bit and gulls cluster around the sodden, half-buried net that hangs from a volleyball post. Backs turned to the wind, their feathers ruffle like poodle curls. Their feet look purple on the cold sand. They all stare up at a kid in a tight hoodie who is draped over the rail, his cargo shorts, halfway down his bum, revealing in the streetlight bright red satin boxers. The kid has a bucket of hot chips that he's stuffing into his mouth.

Chuck them some, Matt thinks.

On cue, the kid throws a chip. Birds erupt in an explosion of screaming. A one-legged gull stands apart, its beak imploring like a laughing clown. Matt uses up the last couple of shots on the film. He might be able to do something with them.

Reloading the camera, he hears shouting. An angry male voice, rising, falling, words he can't make out. He puts the camera away and walks back to the steps.

People are gazing in the direction of the pavilion. One figure is walking quickly towards it. Matt sees bright red plastic beneath the overhead light. Shelly. Catching her up, he sees that what she is wearing is a kid's Little Red Riding Hood raincoat. Funny, he thinks. Probably an op-shop score.

'Hey, Shelly?'

She jumps at his touch. The hood is down and there's no sign of that dolphin smile. She looks away, clutching the lapels tight to her throat.

'My name's Matt,' he says. 'Not Max Dupain. That was a joke.'

'I know who Max Dupain is,' she snaps. 'I did art at school, too.'

The shouting is close now. One word repeated. *Shelly*!

'You'd better go,' she says urgently, but Bull is already lurching out of the dark, all muscle, alcohol-reek and looming menace. He bellows, 'What are you fuckin doin' talking to my woman?'

Matt steps back, aware of how few people are still around. Bull follows, clenched fist raised. Shelly grabs his arm and reefs on it, saying, '*Don't*, Bull!'

Bull staggers.

Shelly, her face transformed, snarls, 'Yeah wanker. Treat us like idiots and then fuck off. You think you're the only one who can read a book? Had to hold my mates back that night, after I told them Max Dupain's dead. So what does that make you?'

Bull tries to shake Shelly off. Deftly, she pulls his arm over her shoulder and turns him away. Half pushing, half pulling, she steers him back towards the pavilion, pausing, when she has reached a safe distance, to shout over her shoulder, 'You know what you *should* call yourself, Max Dupain? FIGJAM! Work that out, dead man.'

Matt hears Bull bellow, 'Fig *what*? What the fuck, *what*?' He watches Shelly pull Bull's head down and say something in his ear. Bull turns. Planting his legs to steady himself, he roars. 'Yeah *FIGJAM*! Fuck off, ya fucking faggot'. He howls with laughter as Shelly leads him away.

Matt shivers as he watches them go. He knows what FIGJAM means. *Fuck I'm Good Just Ask Me*. Everyone in Newie knows that track by a Brisbane hip-hop band which got heaps of airplay a couple of years back.

It's a long way in the dark to where his car is parked. Heading up the concrete steps he sees the Isa Brown woman still huddled against the Lifeguard building. Now she has something blue wrapped around her head. A jumper with the sleeves tied around her neck. It makes her look more like a tortoise than a chook. Suddenly he wishes his grandmother was still around. If he could tell her that, she'd laugh.

The old woman has a book in her lap. The torch she is reading by lights her face. Her skin looks grey, although the jutting beak of her nose is hard red from the wind.

'Must be a good book, to want to read it in this cold.'

She looks up, shows him the book. An old hard-back, the covers sticky-taped together.

'Poetry,' she says. 'John Donne. Keeps me warm.'

For the first time, he notices the shopping trolley behind her, stuffed with belongings.

'You shouldn't do that,' she is saying, 'Take pictures of people with that camera of yours. There are copyright issues, you know. You should ask permission.'

He says uncertainly, 'Um, I could print the ones of you, if you want them.'

She laughs, 'To put up on my walls?'

Her eyes are sharp. They crinkle at the corners. Like Gran's, Matt thinks. Eyes that see a lot.

He says, 'Do you need to go somewhere? I have a car.'

She laughs. 'I'll take that as an apology, but I don't like cars. There's a warm enough spot in the Pavilion, now that the crazy loon has gone.'

She gives Matt a long look. 'How good are you with that camera?'

On the verge of answering pretty good, he says instead, 'Still learning.'

'Keep it that way,' she says. 'I'll give you three minutes.'

Matt realises what she's offering. He starts to fiddle with the camera settings, his mind skidding through the variables: bad light, lack of contrast, his inexperience.

'Hurry up, you're wasting time.'

He works on gut-instinct. Moves around her firing off shots.

'Get closer,' she says.

He moves in. She doesn't flinch, even with the flash right in her face.

'Last one.' She leans and stares into the lens, her face filling the viewfinder. Matt flicks off the flash and sharpens the focus on her unwavering gaze, every skin blotch and wrinkle hard-lit by the streetlight.

The hair on his neck prickles as the shutter clicks.

08: 2008 Sage

'Trace, have you tried smudging?'

Cosmo leans amply on CrystlMania's shop counter, examining the back of a cellophane packet. Tracey peers at the thick grey knobs inside and shakes her head.

'Sage Sticks,' Cosmo reads. 'Native American. The smoke gets rid of bad energy. *Cleanse, heal and bless your house*, it says here. Diffuse smoke in all the corners and shadows of your home. Extinguish sticks in an attractive bowl or an abalone shell. Ha, that'll be easy, there should be plenty of ab shell here in the Bay.'

Everything about Cosmo is flamboyant. Her voice and gestures, collaged clothes, crimson-dyed hair, the blue liner on her eyes and her dolly-pink lipstick. Beside her, Tracey feels bleached. Half-listening, she stirs her finger through a bowl of beads on the counter. Blue and green, brown and cream, like miniature planets. Other worlds. The label says *AMAZONITE: Free your inner warrior, tame negativity and anger, promote peace and balance*. Tracey's peace and balance definitely need promoting. She has hit a wall, and that wall is her son, MJ. But smudging?

'Hey Trace, this says that people can be smudged too. Could be your energy needs cleansing.'

For a frozen moment, Tracey imagines wafting magic smoke around her scowling son. No point, she thinks. He already reeks of it.

She's heard a lot about what she needs since Cosmo moved down from Mullumbimby to Port Stephens. Colour therapy, crystals, bitter mixtures. Tracey doesn't come to the shop for any of that. She comes because, despite being complete opposites, it's good to have a friend. And Cosmo's relentless optimism helps Tracey believe she might, one day, get on top of this surviving thing.

Get a friend to help, it says here, Trace. *Perform with full awareness and in a mindful manner.* I can do that. Why don't you come to my place on Sunday? Give it a go?'

Tracey pushes the bowl away.

'I wish I could cope like you do, Cosmo.'

Cosmo stops mid-flow. 'Cope, Trace?' Her face shadows before the cheerfulness reasserts. 'Do you mean the daughter in rehab? Or the husband who ran off with a teenager?'

Cosmo's laugh takes over her body. Pulling a tissue from the stash in her bra she gasps, 'Christ, Trace, got to laugh or you cry.'

Tracey can't laugh. Or say that wasn't what she meant. And she can't ask how Cosmo coped with having a dead child, so that Tracey can work out how to deal with her living-dead one.

The previous day, driving home from Salamander, Tracey had patted her smooth curls and wished she'd called in to Nelson Bay to see Cosmo to show off her new 'do'. She was feeling unusually buoyant. Leesa at Salamander Hair had complimented her natural grey. Mink, Leesa called it, suggesting a treatment, and Tracey for once decided to splash out. To look nice for MJ tomorrow. She still had a few years before she could get the pension, but her shifts at Coles padded out the money her dad, Cyril, left her along with the house, so she could afford little treats. Thanks Dad, she'd thought.

It had been a surprise, Cyril selling the family home in Beresfield to buy up at Bobs Farm. 'Retirement's for fishing, and all the fish are up at Port Stephens,' he'd said on the phone. There'd been no golden handshake to end his forty-seven years of chicken processing at the Steggles factory. Instead, at a farewell afternoon tea, he was presented with a cellophane-wrapped box of frozen Marylands. 'Brought the roof down with my thank-you speech,' he laughed. 'Said it was time for me to get out of there before I was plucked as well.' Over the next few years, Tracey only went out fishing a couple of times with her father, but there were many blow-by-blow descriptions over the phone of the flatties and tailor and bream he caught when he launched his tinny at Soldiers Point, and the blueys and mudcrabs he'd hauled up in his pots from the shallows of Tilligerry Creek.

Until there was a different call.

'Kidney disease, love. The doc says I'm plucked. You wouldn't want to move out here with me, would you? Give your old dad a hand? I reckon things might get a bit sticky as time goes on.'

Sticky was right. Tracey had no idea. Before long Cyril needed bathing and toileting, and dressings for his awful seeping foot ulcer. Special diets and medications, twice-weekly drives into Newcastle for dialysis, and after his amputation, the wheelchair. It was sad, seeing him get weaker and his skinny old body swell, but she hadn't minded caring for him. After years of living alone, she had her dad to talk to every day, and no more juggling shiftwork to pay the rent. The icing on the cake was when Cyril's doctor suggested she should claim the carer's allowance.

It took Tracey a while to get accustomed to owning a house. She kept her dad's things, so in some ways it felt like he was still around. The silence was the hard part. But now MJ was nearly here. A five-day drive from Darwin, he'd said on the phone.

MJ, home. A bubble of pleasure swelled at that thought. But it popped at the memory of MJ storming out of the Mayfield flat.

Twenty-five years ago.

A month before his final exams at school.

Convinced he'd soon be back Tracey had dosed herself with Valium. After three days she went to the police. When they finally listed MJ as a missing person, a journalist from the Herald phoned. Tracey kept that article, with MJ's Year 12 photo, even though the headline 'Local Man Vanishes' made her want to scream, 'He isn't a man, he's barely eighteen.'

Flicking on her right-hand blinker, Tracey had turned onto Marsh Road. Letting the bad thoughts go, she'd checked the drainage ditches alongside the road and was happy to see them full. So much nicer than at low tide, when there was just black mud between the paperbarks and mangroves. But I *should* have seen Cosmo, she thought. To tell her about MJ. Because if it wasn't for Cosmo, and her daughter Kylie, Tracey wouldn't have found out her son was still alive. She remembers that phone call word-for-word. A voice shouting, 'Tracey? It's really you? Same number, still in Mayfield? I can't believe it! It's me, Cosmo,' and when Tracey had said that she didn't know a Cosmo, she heard a gust of laughter, and recognised her friend's voice, saying, 'Of course you don't. It's Rhonda! I always hated that name, so I shunted it.'

They'd met at church. At first, Tracey had avoided Rhonda: too big, too loud. But their boys ended up best mates in primary school, and after Tracey's husband Brendan died, Rhonda had brought around pot after pot of stew.

Only a couple of years later the shoe was on the other foot, and it was Rhonda's boy, Damian, being buried. He was only thirteen. Tracey thought the funeral would be too much for MJ, bring back the sadness of losing Bren, so they stayed home, but the next day she made rock cakes and took them round. Rhonda's husband Ron had taken Kylie to his mother's and Rhonda was alone. She looked dreadful. Even though Tracey felt sad about her friend's boy being dead, she couldn't help but be glad that her son wasn't.

That horrible time got worse.

First Rhonda and her family moved away. Then Father Frank, who'd been such a support after Bren died, was transferred to Western Australia. And MJ changed so much. He was angry and distant and insisted on being called by his initials, which Tracey hated. She had asked the new priest for advice, but all he said was, 'When boys become teenagers we must expect our relationships with them to change.'

Tracey had tightened her hands on the steering wheel, thinking, thirteen years of wondering if her son was dead, then Cosmo's voice shouting, 'You remember Kylie, my little porky? Skinny like you wouldn't believe now and working up in Darwin. She just rang, Trace, and guess who walked into the café and ordered banana pancakes? Your boy MJ.'

MJ hated bananas was all Tracey could think, as Cosmo rushed on about Kylie's childhood crush on MJ and how she'd wondered if his mum still didn't know where he was. Her attention snapped back when Cosmo said, 'She got his phone number, Trace. Asked me to find you. Heart of gold, my Kyls.'

Tracey had turned into her driveway and stopped to check the mail. The box was empty. MJ was thirty-one when I made that first phone call, she thought, returning to the car. And in the twelve years since, then there's been little more than a gruff voice when I called for Christmas, birthdays. But at least he answered. At least he was there.

But why has he decided to come back, now?

She'd driven on, through the thicket of casuarina trees that bordered her block, and gasped. There was a battered Landcruiser parked near the house.

Five days, MJ said. But it had only been *four*.

Scrambling from the car, she'd shouted his name. Nothing. She turned a full circle. Was he hiding? Some sort of joke? Nothing.

When she heard something clatter, the sound coming from the back of her house, she hurried down the side path. And stopped short at the sight of the broken plants and pots strewn across the paving beneath the pergola. The shelves where they'd sat alongside Cyril's work shed were empty.

Would a possum do that? A python?

The sound of gushing of water led Tracey to the far side of the shed. There was a stranger standing at the concrete troughs. Both taps were turned on full.

It took breathless seconds for Tracey to see MJ in that slouching body, the stubble-clipped hair. She had walked towards him, raising her arms to bridge the lost years. Hugging him, she breathed not air into her lungs, but her son.

'You could have fucking looked after Pop's plants.'

Tracey pulled back as if he had bitten her. Wordlessly, she'd watched MJ pull two streaming plants from the trough, put them on the ground and plunge in two more. Bubbles rose and popped. She pictured drowning kittens.

When her breathing steadied, she said flatly, 'I need help with the shopping.' And turned away.

Dumping the shopping bags on the kitchen bench, Tracey listened to MJ's footsteps behind her and thought, My son, who can hug a slab of beer but won't hug me.

'Where d'you want these?' His voice hard.

She pointed to the laundry. 'Put some in the freezer. They'd be cold if I'd known you'd arrive today.'

'Fast trip.'

In the bedroom with flowery yellow curtains and a single bed, hers until she moved into her dad's room, she slid the wardrobe door open.

'The bed is made up, and there's space for your stuff in here. That box on the top shelf is full of things of yours I've kept. You might want to go through it.'

'Should've just burnt it.'

'That's your job, not mine. I'm making tea. Do you want one?'

'Coffee. Black. No sugar.'

The coffee made, Tracey called out, 'It's ready.' Leaving the mug on the bench beside a plate of sliced Coles' fruitcake, she had taken her tea into the living room and sank gratefully into the familiar contours of Cyril's armchair. Beyond the window there was a kookaburra pecking savagely at something in the overgrown grass. Tracey had tried to keep up with the mowing and watering, but caring eventually took all her time, and when Cyril died, so did her energy. It's a mess out there, she'd thought guiltily, but I've never been a gardener. Not like Dad. And it's hard to look after everything by yourself.

Swivelling the chair to look at the bank of family photos that her dad had framed, before he became too frail, she'd gazed at the blow-up of a snap she'd taken of Brendan and Marty at Bar Beach. Side-by-side in wave-wash, they were oblivious to the big wave that would knock them down like skittles while she stood laughing. That was 1976, their last summer together. Tracey's eyes brimmed. She missed those days in the seventies when men wore their shorts skimpy, and their hair long. Bren had looked like the singer Peter Frampton, and their boy was a mini-Bren.

Beside the beach shot was Tracey's favourite: a school photo of her son as a grinning sixth-grader, with his dreamy blue eyes, freckle-sprinkled nose and white-blond curls to his shoulders. Before she could stop herself, she had pictured those blond curls scattered on lino. It was the summer after they'd lost Bren, and passing the open bathroom door she'd seen her son hacking at his long hair with a knife. His head covered in ugly tufts.

The glare when he saw her in the mirror.

MJ had that same look, out by the trough, Tracey thought, swiping at her tears. His eyes hard and accusing.

MJ sits at his grandfather's workbench under the shade of the pergola. He stretches his legs, still tight from fourteen-hour days of driving from Darwin. Tennant Creek, Winton, Lightning Ridge, Port Stephens. Nothing to do but stay awake, avoid the roos, and remind himself how fucking stupid he'd been to tell Tracey he was coming.

Should've found a cheap pub in Newie.

Never thought there'd be a good reason to be back this way.

Holding a dwarf tree upside down, he checks the bonsai book beside him. Muttering *wakajishi*, he opens a flat wooden box embossed with Japanese characters. Last night he and his mother barely spoke. This morning, she left out stuff for breakfast with a note saying she'd been called in to work. Beside it was the key to Cyril's shed.

It's like a shop inside the shed. The old chicken-plucker didn't hold back when it came to kitting-up. Boating, fishing and gardening gear, and pretty much every tool known to man, methodically stacked on shelves or consigned to drawers. Dozens of books, too. The most thumbed are *Fish Port Stephens* by a bloke called Stinker Clarke, and the ones on bonsai.

Frowning with concentration, MJ uses the delicate steel shears to clip the small tree's tangled root ball. Pop's big hands held these little shears. Visiting the Beresfield house as a kid, he'd followed his grandfather everywhere. Watching him weed and plant, work delicately on his bonsai. Now the box of bonsai ornaments sits beside him on the table, miniature bridges, animals, people. He picks up the ornament that had been his favourite, an old fisherman with a big hat, long white hair and beard, and a tiny red fish dangling from his pole. But the fish is missing, and one side of the broad-brimmed hat has broken off. MJ remembers the Beresfield house as suburban, ordinary, with not a speck of dust inside despite Nan's overload of religious ornaments and pictures of Jesus and Mary. Pop's big shed, with his tinny and tools, was also kept neat, but his garden had been a riot of flowers and fruit and veggies. Probably all bulldozed for a factory by now.

It's funny that Pop didn't bring any of Nan's stuff out here, to Bobs

Farm. The one religious thing in the house is Tracey's old bleeding-heart Jesus, hanging on the wall in his room.

MJ checks the book again and holds the tree above a rectangular, blue-glazed dish to gauge the root-spread. He never worked out what caused the big family fall-out. He doubts Pop was the problem, so maybe it was Nan. She didn't say much, just cooked and cleaned and sewed. He remembers unwrapping the black and white Maitland Pumpkin Pickers jumper she made for his tenth birthday. Before the big lunch she'd prepared. Roast chicken, one of the seconds that Pop used to get cheap from Steggles. Over lunch the adults had talked in low voices about the priests. His dad became upset and Nan got up suddenly and cleared the dishes. When she brought out the cake, a sponge with strawberry jam and cream and ten candles all lit, she said a word that made his dad shout and leave the room, and his mum started crying. There'd been no cake after that, and no grandparents.

MJ still remembers the word his Nan said. *Blasphemy*. The first time Tracey phoned him, she told him Nan had died of cancer.

Maybe if he'd gone to live in Beresfield with his grandparents, he wouldn't have taken off like he did. He'd considered asking, but the thought of all Nan's religious crap put him off. Might've had a warm welcome at Berro. There sure as hell wasn't one when he arrived here yesterday, busting for a piss and the house locked. When he saw the miserable-looking lemon tree near the carport it was as if Pop's voice was in his head: 'Great fertiliser for citrus, lad, never waste a drop.' Pop would have loved this big garden and kept it schmick. It's a total piss-off, seeing it overrun with weeds.

MJ reaches for the water mister and frowns. It was the bonsai that did him in, yesterday. He hasn't been that destructive in a long time. But seeing the brown relics in the elegant pots on Pop's shelves, and discovering, out in what should be a mini rainforest, little trees that Pop had lovingly positioned on rocks and along the winding paths, all struggling or dead and the garden choked by weeds, fallen branches, dried tree-fern fronds, had been too much.

All that work, and his mother let it go.

That's why he'd lost it. Started chucking stuff around. It was the little fisherman who stopped him, rolling out from beneath an upended pot. When he picked it up, it felt like he held Cyril in his hand.

The pot had something written in pencil on its base. He made out *Moreton Bay Fig* and instantly he was a kid again, climbing the giant old trees in Islington Park with his best mate Damo, lungs filled with the fig's green pissy smell, sap sticky on fingers and bare feet. Dried moss and white pebbles still clung to the soil clumped around the bonsai fig's miniature buttresses, and its aerial roots hung like brittle hair. It looked past help, until he realised there were dull-green leaves among the dead ones. He'd found the water trough, left it to soak, and started the search for more potential survivors.

This morning, he discovered *Australian Native Bonsai* among Cyril's books, and in it he read that native fig bonsais can cope with defoliating. There were also instructions for pruning and repotting. It was no surprise to MJ that everything he needed was in the shed.

He tamps new soil carefully back around the fig's roots, refreshes the pebbles and mounds some moss that had miraculously re-greened in the trough. The tree's slender branches spread protectively above the little fisherman.

Standing back to admire his handiwork, he relights his half-smoked joint and wonders how he and the old fella would have got on. After Tracey moved here, she'd put Pop on the phone when she ran out of things to say. It was easy with Pop, no expectations, just stories about his garden and fishing. Talking to his mother always felt loaded. It wasn't always like that. She'd been pretty and soft and laughing before his dad died. Most people learn to cope, but not Tracey. By the time MJ bailed, she'd given up trying to find work and pretty much everything else, just slopped around the flat. They'd barely talked, unless you count the fights.

At least she's pulled herself out of that.

He nips the roach tip. He needs to call that Newcastle Herald journalist, let her know he's here. She'd said in the last email that she'd be full on covering the Papal visit. *Calling the Pope to account*, she wrote, adding, *give me a couple of days leeway, I'll make time.*

What's a couple of days, after all these years?

He gives the fig a last mist. At least one positive thing has come out of staying here. It feels good, reconnecting with Pop through this place. Out here with the plants, he feels right at home.

MJ can't stop his legs from trembling. Staring out over Waratah and Georgetown to the vast grey Moly-Cop factory, he draws deep on his joint. The journalist who is meeting him here, on Braye Hill, is prepared to trust him. Something MJ finds rare in women these days. But how the hell can you explain when you meet someone that your tension and anger isn't about them?

Seeing a car approaching up the hill, he extinguishes the roach and pockets it.

Introductions done, the journalist points to the picnic table furthest down the hill. 'Will that be okay?'

They settle with small talk, MJ explaining he'd lived a few blocks down the hill in Waratah and often came up here, to Braye Park, with his dad. 'He'd tell me stuff about the places we could see. Like how the Hexham Bridge was engineered to lift because big boats needed to get upriver. And what cargo was loaded from the different wharves at the port. I've been away from this place for years, but it's all in here,' he taps his forehead. 'Drawn like a map.'

'Your dad still lives in Newcastle?'

He shrugs. 'Died when I was eleven.'

Later, walking with the journalist back to her car, he decides the meeting wasn't as bad as he'd expected. She'd let him talk, and he told her everything. No stuffing around, no judgements, no bloody sympathy, Intense though. Exhausting. How does she cope with it, he wonders. Story after story. The catastrophe of lives derailed.

As if reading his mind, she says, 'Survivor stories like yours are important, MJ. The key to justice. And letting me use yours now is perfect timing, every newspaper leading with stories about the Pope visiting Sydney for International Youth Week. We need to make it very clear that this Diocese, Maitland-Newcastle, has been one of the nation's worst perpetrators. The extent and flagrance of the child abuse, the Church's refusal to act, priests uncensured, and foisted on other parishes, even sent interstate. Or some,' her tone darkens, 'set up comfortably on a remote church property to do 'admin', as if being out of sight would keep them away from children.'

MJ stares. 'He's still out there?'

She fumbles in her bag for the car keys. Finds them. Hesitates.

'MJ, I think I should tell you this. When I read your first email I was struck by your surname, because it was a name already in my files. Another victim, a man in his fifties, recently gave me a list of other boys from his school that he knew were abused. Childhood friends he'd lost touch with but still worries about, others that he knew had taken their own lives. The dates seem about right. Was Brendan Liffey your father?'

Tracey clutches her tea mug to her chest and sinks into Cyril's chair. She's tired, but six extra hours on the cash register at Coles is better than hours of tension at home.

MJ's Landcruiser is parked outside but there was no answer when she knocked on his bedroom door. He'll be out the back. He's done a lot out there in a short while. The pond and paths have emerged from the weeds, there's bonsai back on the shelves, even a compost heap near the old incinerator. She'd gone out there a few times, to admire the work he was doing, but MJ had barely acknowledged her, so she doesn't go now when he's there.

Not for the first time, she wonders why he bothered to come.

At least dinner times have improved a little. The beer relaxes him. Last night he talked about Darwin and prawn fishing. Nothing personal, but it was better than silence.

It's hard, always worrying she'll say the wrong thing, like this morning. He said he was going in to Newcastle and she answered without thinking, 'Catching up with friends?'

The glare before he turned away.

What was wrong with saying that? He grew up there, surely there's someone he'd want to see. So much anger. He was so bright and easy when he was young, cheerful, caring, the one light in her world after Brendan died.

Turning for the reassurance of the photos on the wall, she gasps.

'*MJ*?'

Her shout echoes through the house. Pushing herself up from the chair, she freezes at the click of his bedroom door.

He stands beneath the living room arch.

She says shakily, 'Your school photos, MJ, where are they? Did you take them?'

'Yep.'

She sinks back with edgy relief. 'You did? Are you fixing something?'

'Yeah, they're fixed. I burnt them. And the stuff you saved in that box.'

Tracey yelps like a kicked dog.

'*Burnt* them? Why would you *do* that? They weren't yours to burn, MJ. They were all I had left of when you were my loving little ...'

'I'm not your loving little anything. Those days are long gone.'

Tracey stares at him, thinking, I want my child back. I don't know who you are, with your snarl and your awful stubbly head, your reek of marijuana.

MJ walks over and thrusts something at her. She shrinks in recognition. A grinning space-suited monkey driving a rocket ship across a starry sky. Red foil letters announce *12 TODAY, WHAT A BLAST!*

'Open it.'

Tracey shakes her head.

'Fucking open it.'

She whimpers, 'I don't want to.'

He leans close and says quietly, 'Read out what my dad wrote. Then tell me how I could come home from a perfectly normal day at school, to be told the perfectly healthy father I had hugged goodbye that morning, was gone. Heart attack, you said. Died in the hospital.'

Tracey's face is in her hands.

'Funny the signs you miss when you're a kid.' MJ's voice is strained. 'Too young to know better, you trust everyone. So, when you are up for it, Mum, please explain to me how my dad was so organised that when he *died suddenly*, two months before I turned twelve, he'd already bought this card, put twenty bucks inside, and written that he loved me.'

Cosmo empties the ash from the abalone shells over the roots of the giant rubber tree outside her flat. When she had to leave Mullumbimby, after the split with Ron, her sister had thrown her the lifeline of the job managing her shop, CrystlMania, and this flat beneath her house in Corlette. It's been hard to make the pokey little space feel like home, she thinks. Upstairs, my sister looks out over the whole Port Stephens estuary, everything sparkling, but when I walk down those back stairs it's a cold descent into shadows, and from inside all I can see through the glass doors is this bloody feral tree swallowing the sky.

The smudging has been a dud, she thinks sadly. If I was still in my pole house on that lovely hill outside Mullum, I'd be surrounded by women you could talk to about almost anything and end up laughing. Up that way rituals like this were a hoot, the singing and affirmations, the whole vibe positive. But Trace is different. We probably wouldn't be friends if our boys hadn't connected. I should have dropped the smudging plan when Trace arrived so upset about MJ and the photos, but I blundered on, telling her she would feel so much better with the negative energy gone.

Cosmo wrinkles her nose at the lingering smoke-smell, as she walks back inside. Tracey sits glumly on the couch, fiddling with the fringe of the sun-face throw-over that Cosmo borrowed from the shop, to cheer the room up a bit.

'Feel like a cuppa Trace?'

Tracey doesn't look up. 'Tea please. Just black.'

Trace didn't come here to be smudged, Cosmo thinks, busying herself in her tiny kitchenette. She came to be told what to do. That's a Catholic upbringing for you. We were trained to be followers, not questioners. Well, I can dish out loads of sympathy, but if Trace won't open up, what hope is there?

She bends to her half-size fridge for the milk. Out of the blue, Tracey says, 'I miss the Church, Cosmo.'

Cosmo knees the fridge shut. 'Jesus, Trace. Where did that come from? You said you haven't gone to Mass for years.'

'Perhaps I should go back. There's always someone to listen and give advice. The priests were so kind when we lost Brendan. MJ and I wouldn't have managed back then, without Father Frank.'

Cosmo snorts. 'Francis Malone?'

Tracey looks bewildered. 'You liked him too, Cosmo. It seemed so stupid, that he had to go to Western Australia when we needed him right here in Newcastle. For years I hoped they would bring him home.'

Cosmo pours the milk into her mug, dumps in three teaspoonsful of sugar and stirs furiously, but she can't hold back.

'Tracey, don't you read the newspapers, watch the news on TV? Everyone loved Frank Malone? Are you sure about that? Haven't you ever wondered if there was a reason the Church moved him away? And who knows what damage he's done to poor little kids over there in the west.'

Replacing the milk in the fridge, Cosmo hears a gargling sound. Tracey's hand is clutched at her throat. Her face is distorted.

'Bloody hell, Trace.'

Cosmo knocks the sugar jar as she rushes to help. It crashes behind her on the floor.

'Was that paper bag a joke?' Tracey's voice still sounds breathless.

Cosmo, squatting awkwardly to sweep up glass and sugar, rocks back on her haunches.

'This hasn't happened to you before, Trace? You hyperventilated. Too much oxygen in your lungs. The bag helps you breathe back carbon dioxide to push it out.'

'How do you know that?'

Cosmo shrugs. 'Panic attacks.'

'*You* have panic attacks?'

'Is the Pope a Catholic?'

Sometimes I can make her laugh, but not this time, Cosmo thinks as she dumps the debris in the pedal bin.

Eyes closed, Tracey slumps back against the cushions. Her chest rises with slow cautious breaths. Cosmo knows that fear of ever trusting your lungs again. Poor Trace, she thinks. All that excitement about her boy coming home and now she's a mess. Kylie might give me grief, but she's never angry like MJ. She would never consciously hurt me.

It strikes her that neither she nor Tracey have been honest about their children. Trace talks up MJ getting labouring work with a mate, or picking mangoes, or catching barramundi, when between the lines every shred of news has been given begrudgingly, and I rave to her about Kylie throwing in hospitality to get a different qualification from TAFE, when what I'm really thinking is, will she get there this time, or give up and slide into another spiral? Do we do that to protect our children, Cosmo wonders. Or to protect ourselves?

She hoists herself onto her only bar stool.

'Trace, I need to tell you something.'

Tracey opens her eyes. She looks hopeful.

Cosmo takes a deep breath.

'There are things you have to know if you don't want to feel helpless, Trace. That's something I've learnt from Kylie. And I couldn't help her until I understood that. Kyls is a fighter, although it's hard for people to see that. She'd get clean, then start to use again, and when people heard she'd relapsed, they would dismiss her as hopeless.'

Tracey pushes herself straighter. 'I don't think of Kylie as hopeless, Cosmo.'

'I'd be the last to blame you if you did. I used to. It never seemed to end. But now I know why. Because I asked her. Kyls told me that when she's straight, she thinks too much about what happened to her brother. The drugs help her cope with the guilt.'

'Guilt?' Tracey looks confused. 'Why would Kylie feel guilty? She was only young. She wasn't there when the accident happened.'

'The accident,' Cosmo says dully. 'A kid who can swim goes off by himself and drowns in a dam. Not even an inquest. They didn't bother back then, and we didn't ask, Ron and I. We were too numb. Just believed what the police told us. Skylarking, they said. Probably met with some local lads. But why by himself, Trace? Without MJ?'

Tracey flinches but Cosmo can't stop now.

'I mean, it's possible. You remember my Damian, Trace? Big and a bit boofy, a clown, didn't always think first. But he was a good kid, and he wasn't stupid. Kyls is sure he was depressed. It took her a while to realise, but before it happened, she'd seen him in his room hitting his head with his fists. He'd screamed at her to leave him alone, so she did. She was scared. Now she wonders if he meant to end up in that dam that night. I can't bear that thought Trace, but it's worse for Kyls, because she thinks that if she'd told me or Ron, he might still be with us. She was only ten, Trace. It wasn't up to her. It was up to me and Ron. Why didn't we realise something was wrong?'

She fumbles in her bra for a tissue. 'All I know is that I let both my kids down. Those bloody priests! Your Father Frank!'

Tracey is shaking her head.

'Cosmo, how can you say that? Father Frank *helped* us.'

Cosmo raises her voice.

'Tracey, listen to me. Francis Malone and that other one, they were in charge when our kids stayed out at that place. They were meant to look after them. So why did my boy drown alone, with not even MJ to help him? Weren't they inseparable? And soon after, Father Frank left Newcastle. Why? If everyone liked him so much? What if something else was going on? It's all coming out now, what priests have done to little kids. Terrible stories. We can't ignore them.'

Tracey pushes herself from the clutch of the couch.

Clambering off the stool, Cosmo says, 'No, Trace, please don't leave. We need to talk this through. You trusted Father Frank. I did too. We trusted all of them. They were our *priests*. How could we have known what was going on back then?'

Tracey, her hands held up like a barrier, backs towards the door.

Cosmo follows her out. Hugging herself against the chill, she watches Tracey climb the stairs. Beyond her, the sunlit garden is so bright it's almost blinding.

'Maybe MJ will talk to me about that night, Trace,' she calls. 'Could you please ask him for me?'

Tracey, clutching the balustrade, looks down.

'MJ wasn't with Damian when it happened, Cosmo, because he was in the bunkhouse, asleep.'

'That's what he told the police, Trace. A scared little kid.'

Tracey bolts up toward the light. But with each step on the stairs, she hears herself saying, 'I don't believe you.' The same words that her mother had said to Bren on MJ's tenth birthday, all those years ago.

Cosmo shouts behind her, 'You've never been one to ask questions, Trace. But you should ask MJ why he burnt his school photos. Maybe that's what he wants you to know.'

MJ glances up at Mount Vincent, a beacon of those trips, thirty years ago, when Father Frank first drove him and Damian to Aberdare for the camp-out weekends. There are new housing estates circling Kurri Kurri but the main street, where he stopped by to go to the hardware and bottle shops, felt much the same. Now his thoughts are fixed on Albert O'Gorman. The Ogre Man, Damo called him, back when Albie seemed harmless and they thought the name was funny.

Slowing the car, he turns off the bitumen. The same dirt road, the same tangled bush. But the pillared gateway he eventually sees, and the mown lawns and circular drive with a rose garden blooming at its centre, are new. Ah, Albie, MJ thinks, now you've tamed the wild as well. Vines drape the verandah of the house as if to hide a secret. He eases the Landcruiser into a marked car park and climbs out. Clicking the door carefully shut, he is startled by the shriek of a cockatoo.

An elderly man answers his knock. His round face is wrinkled, and a fluff of white hair fringes the dome of his head. Put him in a cassock, and he'd pass for a geriatric Friar Tuck, MJ thinks. He swallows the acid in his throat.

'Hello Albie.'

The old man looks blank. 'I'm sorry, should I know you?'

Seriously? Could he really have forgotten? MJ, taken aback, says his name.

The practiced smile flickers.

'It has been a long time, Albie. I used to come out here to see the aviaries.'

A moment's hesitation before the priest's face lights up.

'Ah, the birds? You were a buyer? Sadly, I had to let the business go. As Proverbs tells us, the glory of young men is their strength, and grey hair the splendour of the old.'

The same high-pitched laugh.

MJ forces a smile. 'I thought I heard a cockatoo as I arrived.'

'Oh yes, a few cantankerous old things no one wanted.' Albie's expression alters subtly. 'I couldn't let them go. You'd know that birds caged for a long time can't be set free. They'd never survive.'

He's playing me, MJ thinks. He says softly, 'Birds and boys, still locked in our cages. Were there too many of us, Albie? Too many boys to remember all our names?'

Pretence vanishes. The old man shrills, 'This is church property. You should leave, now!' He tries to close the door but MJ pushes against it. The priest pulls a mobile phone from his cardigan pocket as he retreats along the hall. Following, MJ lets him jab a few buttons before he grabs it, saying, 'Leave that for now, Albie. We can call for help later.'

The study looks the same. The polished timber desk, the wall of locked cupboards that MJ wondered about as a child. Now he's gut-positive that their contents will make irrelevant whatever the priest confesses or denies.

Pulling zip ties from his jacket pocket he pushes Albi into his office chair.

Restrained by the wrists, the old priest glowers at MJ's request for the cupboard keys.

'What about in here?' MJ says, opening the desk drawers. Neat trays of stationery, church-related receipts and quotes, meeting minutes, letters. Riffling through the paperwork, he asks casually, 'Do you remember Damian, Albie?'

The priest looks away.

'I want you to remember him, Albie. Wasn't it your suggestion, that I bring a friend to the bunkhouse sleepovers, so my mum wouldn't worry? Damo was that friend. Two boys for the price of one, double the fun. Remember that mine you told us was forbidden? I was a kid who did what he was told but not Damo, he was fearless. He convinced me and we explored it many times. But you'd understand that, wouldn't you Albie? You know fear and adventure go hand in hand, and that something denied becomes more attractive. It's how you priests operated. How you lived your hypocritical bloody lives.'

MJ abandons the key hunt and fires up the computer. 'What about the password, Albie. You'd be kind enough to give me that?'

No response.

Sitting on the desk, MJ says conversationally, 'You'd know all about the Papal Mass for World Youth Day in Sydney, next Sunday? Of course you do, there's sure to be an invitation here somewhere. A pity you'll miss it. And you'd also know about the Newcastle Herald's call for a Papal apology to the church's child victims? And the journalist who's been campaigning for a Royal Commission? It's all stacking up, isn't it. I met her in fact, a few days back. And I told her about two kids who felt special because their priests treated them like favourites. I didn't hold back, especially about what happened to Damo. Yesterday I told his mother too, and mine. Can you imagine the shock? The guilt that they feel, because they didn't suspect? The grief? My story is going to be on the front page of tomorrow's paper. Compelling reading and no stopping it. It's your story too, Albie. Yours, Frank Malone's, and those evil fucking mates you had.'

The priest shrivels in his chair as MJ walks over to him.

'Priest of the True Sanctuary, Albie,' MJ says quietly. 'Words like that stick in kids' heads when they hear them every week. Damo and I thought the Church would keep us safe. I'm thinking about taking you on a little visit, out to the old colliery you told us not to go to. Maybe a symbolic baptism in the dam for a taste of what Damo went through, before a glimpse of eternity down the mineshaft. That could be your True Sanctuary, Albie. Deep in the dark and forgotten. Unless you help me out.'

MJ enters the password into the computer. Opening the search page, he clicks on the History Log. The first image he pulls up is shocking, but the next few are worse. Taking a thumb drive from his shirt pocket, he inserts it in the machine, opens a new email. He calls up the address he needs, types a brief message, attaches a document from his thumb drive and a copy of some of the images he found and set up in a grid. With the email sent, and the grid of images left up on the screen, he turns back to the priest.

'All done, Albie, all done. I'd already prepared my statement for the police, but those photos of you and the kids will provide context. Maybe you'd like to give your statement direct? Do you want to call them now?

Albie's eyes are fixed on the floor. He shakes his head.

MJ makes the call for him.

It is evening before MJ, carrying the six pack of beer he'd bought earlier that day, gets to the dam. Sitting cross-legged on the bank, he stares at the water. Beyond it, the colliery's derelict chimney stack and winding house rear against the sky.

The place still spooks him the way it did that first time, with Damo. In the early dawn light, with mist rising from the ground, the collapsed roof and crumbling three-storey high arched windows had looked like a set from a horror movie. Inside, they found a chaos of weeds, and broken glass and bricks, and MJ can still hear his high-pitched kid's voice shouting to Damo that the rusting machinery looked like the decaying corpses of huge prehistoric beasts. Later, when they found an old mine shaft, with its mouth blocked by rotted timbers, they had thrown rocks through the gaps. The sounds of falling had lasted a long time.

MJ flicks his joint-end towards the water. The tiny heat-missile arcs and snuffs. He and Damo had shared the best and worst of childhood. How different would life have been if they'd grown to adulthood together? Remained friends. Someone else who knew.

The sky has almost drained of colour. A breeze ruffles the dark reflection of the colliery winding house. As the ripples spread closer, MJ has the sense of the building reaching for him, the way men who he trusted, and some he never knew, had reached for him and Damo as children. Their rough hands, their smell, their weight. The disbelief and pain. Over and over.

He ducks at a sudden rush of air over his head. A slow flapping, that swoops across the water towards the ruins. Some sort of owl, or maybe a bat. Something that can fly free.

MJ thinks of the cockatoo he'd heard screech earlier at the Priest's house. The old birds, unsaleable, unwanted, what will happen to them? He could come back, bring cages. Would anybody care, or even notice if he took them? But then what? He'll be heading back to Darwin.

Maybe I could leave them with Tracey, he thinks. Something for her to look after when I'm gone.

Too tired to follow the thought any further, he listens to the frogs croaking in the reeds. One call, more a click than a croak, reminds MJ of when he and his parents still lived in their house in Waratah, and he sometimes woke in the night to the click of the back door, the creak of a floorboard. If he called out, his dad's shape would appear at his bedroom door.

'Couldn't sleep, kiddo. Been out for a walk.'

Thinking time, his dad used to call those dark nights he spent on Braye Hill, although he called it Brave Hill, with a lop-sided smile to make it seem funny. But it wasn't a joke. That must have been the place his dad went to, trying to hold himself together.

Later, hearing kids at high school laughing about Braye Hill being a poofter hang-out, MJ had wondered for a while if the break-up with his grandparents had happened because his dad was gay.

Now there's another story.

He cracks a can of Tooheys and takes a deep swig. The beer's warm, but he's beyond caring.

After Tracey read out what was written in the birthday card, he told her what the journalist said about his dad's name on the list.

'So, there was no heart attack?'

Tracey had shaken her head.

'And that fight with Nan and Pop? Our last time at Beresfield? Dad told them what the priests did to him as a kid?'

'Your Nan wouldn't listen. She refused to believe it.'

'What about you, Mum? Did you believe him?'

Tears had rolled down her cheeks. 'I should have. If I had, he might still be here. I am so sorry, MJ.'

Gullible, like her mother, MJ thinks.

Hidebound by religion.

Innocent.

Raising his beer to the oncoming night, he shouts, 'This one's for you, Dad.'

Pinpricks of starlight tremble on the water. The frog calls have swelled to a deafening chorus.

MJ drains the last beer and decides that the deepest croak sounds like, *the martyr, the martyr.* Sure to be a little frog, he thinks. The smallest ones have the biggest croak.

He wonders if life would have been better as a frog. Nothing to do but eat, swim, sing for sex, die of old age. Or slide down the gullet of something stronger. Predator or prey, you croak either way.

The laugh dies in his throat as memory swamps him: his breath rasping as he followed Damo along the dark bush track, running for the old mine, somewhere to hide. The car's headlights swinging across the dam's surface and then behind him, so his shadow was flying ahead. But not fast enough. Damo turning to yell 'Get off the track,' his face a wild-eyed white mask. Dodging through saplings lit by the car lights, tripping and falling with no breath left in him. The slam of a car door, the sound of feet pounding. Being dragged to his knees, the sweaty arm pulled tight around his neck, the hot hand clamped over his mouth, the voice snarling, 'Shut up, you little prick' as the car drove on.

Sudden quiet, until another man started shouting, and Damo was screaming '*Fuck off, fuck off.*'

The splashing in the dam had gone on and on and on.

Sobs wrack MJ's chest. He is a terrified child, huddled on the couch in Albie's living room, while a huge policeman asks questions about what happened during the night, and Albie sits intent as a hawk across the room, making sure that he stuck to the script: he'd slept all night in the bunkroom and knows nothing.

It's over now, MJ tells himself. But how can it ever be over?

Slowly, he pulls off his boots and socks and places them beside the empty beer cans. He stands, strips off his clothes, folds them on top of his boots.

He steps into the dam gingerly, the water cold, the mud rank-smelling. It squeezes between his toes and sucks greedily as he pulls each foot free.

Ripples shush into the rushes. The frogs stop calling.

The water is almost to his chest when he feels another rush of air above him. He wades deeper, following the bird's dark flight towards where the tall chimney stack of the colliery points like a finger to the sky.

09: 2009 Protection

The Troop Carrier judders over the rutted sand track as the dingoes lope ahead through the long morning shadows. Six golden females following their leader. The *she-team*.

The vision fades, but those potent words, she-team, remain in Jazz's mind like a mantra.

She's been back in Newcastle for seven months. She misses Alice Springs, and the desert communities she worked with during her intern year, but she'd missed home more. When a full-time casual contract came up at the Central Women's Support Service, work in the city that had raised her *and* in the field that she loves, she'd applied. It is still hard to believe that she got the job, and now, she thinks, Hanny's been talking about a new full-time permanent position being created, and if my boss has already mentioned that directly to me twice, couldn't that suggest she's letting me know that she thinks I'm ready to take on becoming a real part of *her* she-team?

Jazz is convinced that her future *should* be with this organisation. She is not as experienced as the rest of the staff, but she is positive that she is as passionate as they are about helping vulnerable women and children. But it has still been a shock, learning the extent and complexity of need in the city which, for the bulk of her twenty-four years, has cushioned her with sunshine and great beaches, parties, pubs and music gigs, and the warmth and security of her family and friends. Sure, when she took this work on, she'd expected to deal with domestic violence and mental illness and heaps more. But she hadn't anticipated the sheer extent of the poverty and homelessness, the child abuse, and the disadvantage faced by First Nations' people, and how hard it could be for refugees trying to adapt in a country and culture so alien.

So many needing so much. That's the hidden side of Newcastle, she thinks. It has been confronting to realise that she really hadn't known her city at all.

Hearing a tap on the wall outside the open door of her office, Jazz calls, 'Hello! Come on in!'

No one fills the space.

'Aamira? Is that you?'

Aamira peers shyly around the door frame. 'The time is wrong? I am too early?'

Aamira's appearance at Jazz's door is always breathtaking. The riot of African patterns and colours she wears, so vivid against her dark skin. And the scarves she twists adroitly around her head, so flamboyant that it's easy to miss the machete scars that corrugate one side of her face.

Tall and impossibly slender, Aamira steers the stroller past the comfy lounge near Jazz's desk, choosing one of the wooden chairs that sit against the wall. Jazz gazes at Happiness, fast asleep in her stroller. Her round breast-fed cheeks and knots of glossy black curls, her satiny limbs beneath the frills of a pink nylon dress. So beautiful it is hard to look away.

'How are you going, Aamira?'

Straight-backed, her eyes downcast, Aamira whispers, 'I am fine, thank you.'

Jazz knows that Aamira is not fine. She was recently raped again by a man in her boarding house. A man who is also a refugee, and from Aamira's home country. The man who fathered Happiness.

Aamira, at forty, hadn't wanted a child. She hadn't wanted attention from any man. So Jazz thinks that the name she chose for her daughter speaks volumes. But her countryman kept returning to her door, demanding sex. Despite Aamira and Happiness being safely housed in a refuge now, Jazz is convinced that the only way to protect them properly is to take them to the police station, where she can take out an AVO against the man. For weeks now, Aamira has been softly resisting and Jazz can't understand why.

Studying her client's gaunt profile, her beautiful sharp-as-a-sickle cheekbone, Jazz has a sinking feeling that today will be no different.

She talks over the process again. How necessary it is to report the man. The conditions he will have to observe, ways that the AVO will keep Aamira and Happiness safer.

'I can take you there this morning, Aamira. I promise I'll be with you every step of the way.'

Aamira, her head bowed, and holding the photograph she always brings in between her palms like a prayer, says quietly, 'But you will not step beside me each day and each night. The Police will not step beside me.'

Baulked, Jazz tries the one way she knows that might circumvent Aamira's retreat.

'Will you let me look at your photo again?'

The photo is very creased. It shows a cluster of round mud huts with conical thatched roofs, some stunted trees, a scatter of scrawny chickens. A goat is tethered beside the closest hut, and beside the goat three small, beaming, skinny-limbed children hug each other tightly. Behind them, a laughing man spreads his arms in an air embrace. Aamira's husband and children. Massacred, Jazz knows, as Aamira walked home from her day's work in the township an hour away. When she arrived, the attackers were still there.

Jazz stares at the photo while Aamira quietly talks on about her life before she became a refugee. A twig broom, that Jazz hasn't noticed in the picture before, leans against the wall of the hut, and the bare earth where the children stand, has been swept clean. She can even see their footprints in the thin dust.

Jazz's mind drifts with that image to the day she'd followed dingo pawprints along the sandy bed of the Finke River, the afternoon light as golden as the elusive she-team that she'd hoped to see again. She hears Aamira talking about the coldness of winter in Newcastle, and how isolated she feels when women at the refuge complain about the smell of her cooking, and how hard life is without a village. Lulled by her slow, patient voice, and still partly off with the dingoes, Jazz only comes back to full focus when Aamira is already standing.

'I will go,' Aamira says, taking hold of Happiness's stroller.

Jazz glances at the wall clock, and jumps up. 'Sorry, Aamira, I was distracted. It's my lunch break now and there's a bus in ten minutes. Perfect. I promise you that reporting that man is the best step for you to take.'

Aamira says gently, patiently, 'I do not mean to go to the police station. In my culture a widow must have a protector, and that man says he is my countryman, even though he is not of my people. He says I must marry him, that he only takes what is his right.'

Chilled, Jazz hands back the talisman photo. Usually there is a wistful smile as Aamira tucks the image into her purse, but this time her face doesn't soften.

With Aamira's words about the perpetrator sinking in, Jazz thinks guiltily, Why didn't I already know that? Why did it take Aamira so long to tell me? I can't let her go like this.

Shuffling through the papers on her desk, she says 'Hang on a minute, Aamira, I have something for you.' Finding the brochure, she says, 'I did this on the weekend. A new coastal walk that's just opened, look, there's a map of it here. It isn't hard, and there are beautiful views. Now that the weather's starting to warm, it might be something you and Happiness would like to do. Being outside is always good for lifting the spirits.'

'The spirits?' Aamira's smile comes briefly back as she takes the brochure.

'Oh, no, not the actual spirits,' Jazz falters. 'I mean being in the sun always makes me feel happier. It might help, don't you think?'

Aamira pushes the stroller and Happiness out the door and the singing colours leave with them. On impulse, Jazz follows. Leaning into the corridor she calls, 'Enjoy the rest of your day, Aamira!' She is rewarded by Aamira giving a smile and a wave before she and the stroller disappear around the corner.

Jazz returns to her chair and checks to see who her next client will be. Time to finish some reporting before they arrive. But the call of the dingoes stays strong. Last year, newly fledged as a psychologist, all the positions that she applied for required previous experience. The one job on offer that didn't, circuit work which involved travelling to remote Aboriginal communities out of Alice Springs, was advertised as an internship. In other words, the most basic of wages. But it also promised excellent supervision and perks like accommodation, and travel costs. Jazz had surprised herself, and her family, by applying for it.

Growing up in Newcastle, Jazz had the usual adolescent dreams about escape. To Sydney or Melbourne, London or Paris, somewhere more glamorous, less gritty, industrial and boring. Central Australia was never on her radar. So, as she descended from the air-conditioned plane to a gritty desert airport and a furnace of glaring air that felt not very different from the heat from the furnace at the Steelworks she'd felt, at a safe distance, on a school excursion, she was sure she'd made the worst decision of her life. Two weeks later that worry flew out the window of the Troopie, as she drove out of town with Beyula, the co-worker with a contagious laugh, who'd been assigned to teach her the ropes of the circuit, and Beyula said, 'So you grew up in a big city? You ready to get your mind blown?

Blown it was. Jazz was overwhelmed by the intensity of colour, the desert's ochre sand, grey green spinifex, the endless red craggy rocks of the Macdonnell Ranges and their indigo shadows, the shouting blue of the sky. She loved the slender desert casuarinas which seemed like watching spirit people, and the welcome in the communities they visited. And the dingoes. They had seeded her mind from the moment Beyula pulled up, as they crossed the dry bed of the Finke River, and pointed out the matriarch and others whose appearance or characteristics she knew by sight. Jazz had asked if they were all females, and Beyula beamed, 'Sure are. That's the she-team!'

From then on Jazz watched out for dingoes wherever she went into the desert. Most sightings were little more than a flicker in the scrub and shadows. But she saw the she-team again, when she was back near the Finke. They were hunting through a tumble of rocks not far from the track, and she'd stopped the Troopie, to watch. They were close enough to pick out individual characteristics: the different shades of brown and gold, the one with a black shoulder stripe, the limping bitch with a clubbed front foot. They'd seemed unfazed as if they'd already absorbed the vehicle's regular appearances into their landscape. The matriarch was unmistakable, older, bigger, powerful-looking, the top of one ear missing and her muzzle crooked by a long scar. Jazz watched her come cautiously towards the vehicle until she was only eight or ten metres away. She'd stood poised and watchful, and Jazz, awed, returned that intense gaze, wondering, ready to bolt, or to attack? But perhaps it was neither. After a few long minutes the dingo simply turned and trotted away.

Hanny has that intensity, Jazz thinks, picturing her boss. She is most definitely the matriarch of this team.

It is mid-afternoon, and six appointments later, when Jazz hears a loud voice in the corridor. She quickly shoves the lunch she has just started on, in a drawer of her desk.

Essie barrels in, white hair damp beneath her green beret, her battered shopping trolley topped with a jumble of books.

'Two dollars the lot,' she gloats, showing Jazz a book on dream analysis by Jung, Doris Lessing's *The Grass is Singing*, and a tome of poems by Pablo Neruda.

'And this one's for you'.

She hands over a dog-eared paperback of Christina Stead's *The Man Who Loved Children.*

'Stick it on your bookshelf. Like an affirmation. The title's ironic of course.'

Jazz laughs and does as she's told.

Essie is a regular visitor. Jazz knows from her file that she has lived rough in Newcastle for nearly twenty years, give or take a few early stints in psych wards. PTS brought on by the earthquake. Fiercely independent, she resists community housing and emergency accommodation because buildings with narrow spaces, like hallways and toilet cubicles, freak her out. Coming to the support service is one of her survival strategies. Converted from a late 1800s police station, it has wide corridors and roomy facilities for client use, perfect for washing herself and her bits of laundry. It is nothing to see her wander into the communal kitchen space, swaddled in one of the supplied towels while all her clothes are in the dryer. The towels stay when Essie drops by, but the mini soaps, hand cleaner and shampoos disappear in bulk. Another of Essie's strategies, if she needs a break from sleeping rough, is to jump the last train to Sydney, overnight on it at Central, and return pre-dawn when the conductors are still dozy. When Jazz expressed reservations about an unsupported woman being on the station or the train late at night, Essie had said, reassuringly, 'Oh, don't worry about that. Some nights there's quite a crowd of us,'

Which, thinks Jazz, settling back into her chair, was not reassuring at all. Casually, she asks, 'Have you seen your sister recently?'

Extracting information that Essie doesn't want to give is like squeezing blood from a stone, but she had recently volunteered that her sister had a space built in the back of her garage. 'It's nice enough,' she'd said. 'I can leave the roller door up, and there's a half-wall between me and her car. She's made a little kitchen and bathroom combined and given me a decent bed, a fan and a heater. She leaves me packet soup and Tim Tams. All that I need.'

Gazing around the office as if there are things she's never noticed before, Essie eventually answers, 'Mai? Not for months. No need, the winter's been mild. Last time I saw her, Kim was there.'

By now, Jazz knows the playfully light way Essie can drop a bombshell.

'Kim?'

Essie looks back, her sharp eyes twinkling in their crepey folds.

'My son. Not really mine, though. I gave him to my sister. Sensible really, he looks like her not me.'

'You have a son? How did I miss that?' Jazz pulls open her file drawer.

'Oh, don't bother, he won't be in there.'

'How old is he? Should I be listing him with Mai as your next of kin?'

'Oh, must be twenty something by now,' Essie is loving this. 'And no, thank you. We're not ready for that.' Brusquely, she changes the subject. 'Now, I didn't come in to bestow on you the pleasure of my company. A generous dentist close to here will pull my tooth at 8am tomorrow. So, now that I'm fresh as a daisy, it would be good to find somewhere clean to sleep in the CBD.'

Essie reads aloud from her Neruda, while Jazz calls the two places in her register that fit that requirement. Hearing that they are both already full, she bounces to her feet and grabs her trolley, saying over her shoulder as she sails off, 'Ah well, the station'll be close enough.

Another train adventure!'

Sitting in the sudden quiet, Jazz can't help comparing Essie with Aamira. How do you help someone who refuses to help herself, she wonders. But a moment later, she floods with shame at her own naivety. Aamira *has* helped herself, over and over again. She survived the attack by the men who killed her family, left the home and the land her people had held for generations, and coped with the immensity of her grief and loss and the years in refugee camps. She is making a life for herself in a totally alien country. And she called the child conceived in the worst way possible, Happiness.

The phone rings. An internal call. Hanny on the line.

'Jazz? Something's come up. Can you give me twenty minutes in my office?'

Jazz arrives at the meeting room late, to find Hanny, usually the first to appear, is still not there. The interview in her office, Jazz thinks, it must be dragging on.

It is late in the day and there's a sense of tiredness. The women spaced around the big table are uncharacteristically quiet, a few chatting softly, others read papers they've brought along or check their phones. She glances at their faces. It has been hard to meet everyone properly, the place is always busy, and people are often out of office. She's got to know most of her colleagues fairly well over the last months, but a couple of the older women still daunt her.

When no one meets her eye, Jazz wonders, has the grapevine already done its job? Have they decided I'm not up for this work? That I can't cope?

It's true, she does feel overwhelmed, often. Days when nothing that she did at uni, the case studies and role-plays, the focus groups and research, the reams of reading and assessments, and not even some of the complicated situations she and Beyula had to sort for people in the desert communities they went out to, prepared her for the sheer volume and complexity of this job. And she's been determinedly, maybe stupidly, independent. Hanny has often reminded her that she works with people with a huge amount of experience, and they are willing to share it. She could have asked someone for advice about Aamira, but she didn't want to risk being seen as lacking.

Tears threaten. She'd give anything to keep working here. She loves the women who've come in, flamboyant characters like Essie, and the solid matter-of-fact women, and women who take weeks of coaxing before they reveal what they have to deal with, even the ones who are so broken they feel no hope. Especially those women. All of them so stoic.

Like Aamira.

This waiting is too hard. Surreptitiously, Jazz wipes her eyes. She turns, for distraction, to the dingoes. But the image that comes immediately to mind is confronting, the time she witnessed the dingo matriarch and two other grey-muzzled females, turn on one of the young dogs, and savage her. When the pack moved on, the young one followed, but a long way back, bleeding and slow.

Jazz's throat feels like sand. The other women in this room are clear about how things should be done, and don't tolerate bullshit. Will they turn on me, teach *me* a lesson? Tell me I'm not good enough to stay with the team?

She hears a loud rumble out in the street, something passing in the regular grind of traffic, and forces her mind to follow it. Outside, people will be enjoying the unexpected warmth, walking beneath the budding trees, looking into shop windows, searching for car-keys. A normal busy day.

Inside, nothing feels normal.

This morning, as Aamira left, she had looked back along the corridor and waved the brochure in the air. Her smile was back, that white, gap-toothed smile that dispelled the shadows and made her look younger, beautiful, hopeful. This morning, when Aamira left, she didn't catch the bus back to the refuge. Instead, she followed the coastal walk mapped on the brochure, pushing her daughter in the stroller four kilometres to Strzelecki Lookout. When they reached the top, she left the stroller behind, and with Happiness in her arms, climbed through the barrier fence, walked to the edge of the cliff, and fell.

Jazz leans forward in her chair to try to stop the ache.

Hanny rushes in. 'Sorry. A hell of an afternoon. Thanks for your patience.'

The women around the table straighten and turn to their leader, alert to whatever will eventuate.

Dropping into the chair left for her, Hanny glances around the room. 'Okay. You are here because you've seen my email with the very sad news about Aamira and little Happiness. And I realise that not all of you had a chance to meet them, but we all experience the shock, and the grief. I will send out a copy of the report I compiled with the police, but you are also likely to see some challenging reports in the media. Best avoided, in my opinion.'

She glances across the table at Jazz.

'Most of you already understand my reason for calling this meeting, but I am not sure that Jazz does. However, I think the best thing we can do for now, Jazz, is to give you the chance to talk through with all of us what has happened. Are you okay with that?

Jazz freezes.

'Do it, Jazz,' Hanny says quietly. 'You'll be fine.'

Across the table, one of the daunting grey-haired women says, 'Jazz, it might help to know that most of us here have had to face up to something like this, some more than once. Aamira made her choice, and it is a terribly confronting one. In times like this we can only remind ourselves that the protection we try to offer is not a guarantee, but what we do our best to aim for.'

The last time Jazz saw the dingoes, their pelts shone red-gold in the late sun as they picked their way carefully between the rocks leading up to a low ridge. They had three little pups in tow. Again, the old female had stayed behind near the Troopie, her eyes intent on Jazz. When her pack was all safely out of sight, she was gone too. But Jazz was left with the absolute certainty that the intensity in the matriarch's yellow eyes was recognition, not aggression.

Looking up, she sees Hanny watching her like that. The other women are too. They are on her side. They want her to learn.

The doubt in Jazz's gut turns to fierceness.

10: 2010 Dog Beach

An angel sits on each of Lyssa Carmody's shoulders.

She has known this since, as a ginger-haired six-year-old, she climbed into the lap of an old woman called Maeve in a nursing home in Forster. Lyssa's mother worked there as an aide, and Maeve was her favourite resident.

Lyssa remembers crying. She remembers Old Maeve wrapping her skinny arms around her and saying, in a voice as soft as her name, the angels would always look over her. She remembers a hairy chin, eyebrows like worn toothbrushes and the smell of mouldy grass.

Sometime later, when Lyssa asked about the angels, her mum said the old woman was Catholic, and her little boy had drowned when he was four.

As if that explained everything.

Lyssa doesn't acquire new manifestations of the angels, they acquire her. She has never actually seen them, not by sneaky sideways glances or catching them out in a mirror, but she knows how they look. Over sixteen years they've run the gamut from rainbow Tinkerbells to white-robed Christmas card angels with creaky pigeon wings, dreamy Chagall-esque lovers, and skinny angular goths with black-ringed eyes, spiked hair, and wings like rusted TV antennae. From Year 10, her senior schoolbooks and folders filled with increasingly dark drawings of them, and she began to wonder what the point of them was. They hadn't saved her from anything, or miraculously increased her IQ. They hadn't made her freckly skin browner and her hair dark, like her gorgeous little half-sister Izzy's. They hadn't stopped her mum from marrying Nige.

The angels' shifts in identity accelerated once Lyssa moved to Newcastle to study art at uni. They began to appropriate different graffiti characters around the city. One settled on a lugubrious character with a coat with a turned-up collar and a brimmed hat pulled low over his yellow eyes and beak of a nose. He calls himself Hawkface. The other segued through an endless range of oddities including David Bowie from the goblin king mural in Hunter Street, before announcing himself, now herself, as Miz Moon. Little more than a round androgynous face over which pastel colours spread like blush, her lips are theatrically pursed and her heavily-lidded sanpaku eyes roll frequently skywards. Her opinions, offered in an irritating squeak, are generally nonsensical.

With the semblance of wings long gone, the angels now feel more like familiars than protectors. Consciousnesses that share Lyssa's internal conversations. Their constancy is, somehow, a comfort. She likes to think they look out for her.

The end of March has trumped a lacklustre summer with a flush of hot days. Lyssa steps from the coolness of the city Art Gallery, where she works two days a week, into the full blast of afternoon sun. Brushing irritably at her shoulders she asks the angels, How come, if you're made of light, you feel so damn humid on my skin?

Fluttering indignantly, the angels settle straight back.

Lyssa darts across sticky bitumen to prop in the deep shade beneath the giant native figs that line Laman Street. She's dismayed to see trenches dug beside some figs' buttresses. The City Council has commissioned root scans, looking for evidence that the trees have reached their use-by date. Lyssa gazes along the street at the green tunnel the canopy creates, and the sculptural pattern of trunks and limbs. These trees are an icon of this city, she thinks. They can't be cut down.

Miz Moon starts to whinny anxiously. Hawkface tells her to shut up, and grinds on about the trees being planted for city pride, and amenity of the workers, and habitat for birds and bats. *But who cares about that these days?* he says. *Not this bunch of politicking twats.*

From the top of the stairs, everything below in Civic Park looks wilted. A couple of kids climb in the clump of Dragon's Blood trees and a red-faced man runs with outspread arms towards a flock of corellas pecking in the grass. There is no sign of the gardens team. More specifically, no sign of the cute-looking new worker who'd joined them recently. Young, tall, black hair tied back, and looking a bit uncomfortable in his still-neat Council getup, he'd gazed her way and smiled a few times when she ate her lunch in fig-tree shade. She's seen him around town, driving an old green Kombi with a yellow kayak on the roof.

Damn, she thinks, I wanted to make a date with that kayak.

What self-respecting worker knocks off late on a Friday?

Yeah. Thanks, Hawkface.

The corellas shriek up in a white cloud.

Halfway down the stairs to the park, Lyssa stops to watch the Captain Cook fountain jet its perfect arcs over the monumental copper forms. The angels ruffle in the spray drift as if their feathers still exist. What did Captain Cook ever do for Newcastle, apart from sailing past with barely a blink, she wonders. Margel Hinder must have thought the same when she submitted her concept to the Fountain Design Prize. The fountain might be named for Cook, but Hinder cheekily made him irrelevant, expressing instead rocks, wind and water, the landscape here as he would have seen it, before the Brits took over and started to wreck the place. Surely it should be called the Margel Hinder fountain. She designed and engineered it. She did the work, welding the forms herself.

Helped by her husband, and other blokes.

Lyssa groans, Give me a break, Hawkface. Would you say that if a male sculptor created something this size and employed extra labour to do it? This city's always been way too damn blokey and women artists need more credit. Hinder should be the one commemorated here.

Isn't it your job, to change that?

Tell me something I don't know.

A bead of sweat trickles between Lyssa's breasts. Thinking about that afternoon's team meeting, how positive everyone was about her proposal for a feminist art trail, she hears the deep-throated rev of an engine. She spins to see her bus pull out of the King Street stop.

Shoulders slumped, she considers her options. A torrid twenty-minute wait to take a hot ride to Carrington, where the closed-in verandah she rents behind an old workers' cottage—blocked from any suggestion of a river breeze by the huge dockside GrainCorp silos—will be like an oven? Or stick to the shady streets and wander down to the waterfront, hoping an afternoon southerly will blow through?

Ignoring the angels' bleats, Lyssa jerks her backpack higher on her shoulders, and heads towards Darby Street.

As she waits in blazing sun for the lights to change, Hawkface notices Finnegans Pub opposite and suggests a cold ale. Miz Moon drops the inane song she's been droning and whines, *A cocktail! Sex on the Beach. With a yellow umbrella.*

Lyssa snaps.

Bloody hell, you two, sort yourselves out. Angels don't have human needs and they sure as hell don't drink.

A moment later the lights go green. Miz Moon mimics the crossing audio with a shrill '*Dick dick dick dick dick*,' and Lyssa is laughing out loud.

Legs dangling, Lyssa sits on a rock below Nobbys Causeway, and stares over the wide river. Upstream, dogs and people run in and out of the water at Horseshoe Beach, and a ferry from Stockton beelines towards Queens Wharf. Behind it a yellow kayak rocks on the settling wake. The late sun turns the whole scene a hazy gold.

Hawkface has gone quiet but Miz Moon has been incessantly whining.

Leave whenever you want, Moon. I can manage without you, Lyssa says crossly. Want a fact about angels? They don't wear lipstick. Want another? I don't even believe in you.

All three jump at a deep horn-blast.

A huge black coal ship is entering the river mouth, nudged from behind by the two guide tugs that Lyssa recently saw race out past Nobbys lighthouse. She watches with a sense of doom as the ship slides like a monstrous slug up the channel. *The Mineral Joyful*, she reads on its bow as it passes. Off to Kooragang for another load of toxic shit to choke the planet. Joyfully destroying the world by stealth.

The ship moves inexorably on. In its path, and dwarfed by its bulk, is the yellow kayak. The paddler appears to make no attempt to move out of its way. The kayak disappears. Miz Moon shrieks, *Left that abatement too late.* Hawkface growls, *Do you always have to be an idiot?*

Lyssa holds her breath.

The kayak reappears. Watching it spear away from the ship towards

Pirate Point, she can't help thinking, Moon's right. Why take that risk?

Staring at the turbid throb of the ship's wake, she thinks of a colonial painting she's seen of Aboriginal men on this river. Standing in their bark canoes, with their fishing spears raised. Because they could see the fish. Because before the disaster of agriculture and mining and industry and these endless shitty coal ships with their churning propellers, the Hunter must have run clear. *Coquun*. That's what Nige calls this river. She remembers him saying, 'That's what my people called it. It means fresh water. Water you could live from. What a river should be.'

Nige, she thinks with a pang. A seriously good stepdad, and so patient. But what a hard time I gave him.

She looks back towards the sea. The river's discolouration continues well beyond the breakwalls. Where she is sitting would be about the same distance from the sea as the bridge up the coast at Forster, but when you look down from that bridge every little detail in the water is clear. Whiting shadows flitting over the sand, bubble trails of diving cormorants, sometimes a sea turtle. Driving across, her mum used to say, 'So many colours, Lyss, describe them for me. Find new ways,' and Lyssa rose to each challenge, her words by high school becoming as fluid as the view. 'Indigo and hyacinth,' she might say. 'Mother-of-pearl, teal and pigeon-breast grey.'

Crossing that bridge on the day of her mum's diagnosis with Izzy fast asleep in her car seat in the back, Lyssa had stared numbly at the water and said, 'Sadness blue.'

There'd been a long silence before her mum replied, 'You could call it that.'

The kayaker paddles rhythmically back towards Horseshoe Beach. Even though it's still too distant to be certain, Miz Moon squeals, *Whoopee-boot, this could be it!*

Could be none of your business, Lyssa, flicks back.

There's a flurry of movement as the kayak nears the shore. A caramel border collie dances on the front hull, its tail a pampas grass plume.

Lyssa hears a distant shout. The boat tips, and the dog leaps out.

Standing waist-deep, the paddler wrings the river from his long hair.

Eeyew, Miz Moon squeaks. *Much dog-shittery*.

Lyssa watches him fan the circling dog with broadside splashes. She smiles. Definitely Kayak-boy.

She stands and brushes her gritty palms against her cotton skirt. As she climbs back to the walkway a familiar voice calls her name. One of her sculpture tutors from uni is doing a Cliff Young shuffle from the end of the causeway. The woman pulls up, and hands Lyssa a large feather.

'Here, you should have this.'

Lyssa turns it in her hand. Strong shaft, blue-grey barbs, a cloud of downy white at the base.

'Sea eagle? Nice. Where'd you find it?'

'Spiralled down in front of me. By the time I'd picked it up the bird was miles away. I kept going, and then I saw you.'

They chat briefly before the woman heads on towards town. Lyssa follows, twirling the feather between her fingers. Nige reckons the sea eagle is his spirit animal. Whenever he sees one, he stops in his hyper-energetic tracks to watch it. Complete focus. As if he can read the bird's every movement.

'Why are you so hard on him, Lyss?'

Mum's voice in her head. So much tension between them over Nige.

Lyssa swings off the causeway and skirts the patch of scrub before Horseshoe Beach. The green Kombi is in the car park, kayak already strapped to its roof. The driver's door open, but no driver. She looks towards the beach. The dripping border collie is returning, its nose glued to footpath smells. Kayak-boy follows, a paddle held loosely on his shoulder. As he crosses the glittering path that the low sun casts over the river, the glare etches his limbs to almost breaking. Shielding her eyes, she thinks of Giacometti's *Walking Man* sculpture. More mirage than substance, only the chemistry of bronze to keep it vertical.

Rusty-can cancer, Miz Moon says tremulously.

With a mental lurch Lyssa is back in the hospital, watching the disease eat her mum away until it seems only sinew and sheer will keep her going.

The urge to talk to Kayak-boy seeps away. Moving out of sight behind a big RV, Lyssa watches him whistle his dog and roughly towel it dry. They climb into the Kombi and drive away.

Bolstered by a couple of cheering drinks with friends at Queens Wharf, Lyssa dawdles home through Honeysuckle in the humid night. She hears distant strains of music. Recognising a riff, she remembers that Fishkicker is playing tonight at the Lass O'Gowrie. She picks up pace and hurries towards the pub.

As she squeezes through the crowd loitering on the footpath, she is hit by the fug of beer and perspiration emanating from inside. Music pounds from the stage and the packed dance floor throbs. Joining the pack waiting three-deep at the bar, she turns to watch.

And there he is. Kayak-boy.

His tanned shoulders bare under green overalls, and his black hair flowing loose, he easily negotiates the jostling space, each movement loose but contained. When Fishkicker's singer grabs his didge and begins to beat box through it, Kayak-boy stops dancing to watch. He stands absorbed, chest heaving. The singer returns to the mic, his powerful voice soaring over the claps and cheers. Kayak-boy swings around, heading for the bar.

Lyssa, still not much closer to ordering, makes room for him. Recognising her, he breaks into a grin.

'Hey!'

Whatever else he says is drowned by the noise around them. Giving up, he mouths 'Drink?' She shrugs, laughs, and mimes pulling a beer tap. There's a hint of his musky soap and sweat scent as he leans across her to signal the barman.

Two schooners appear on the bar mat. He grabs them and cocks his head towards the beer garden.

Outside it's cooler but not much quieter. Lyssa snaffles a just-vacated table by the back wall. She slides along the bench seat, kicks off her shoes and tucks up her feet. Kayak-boy folds in beside her, stretching out his long legs.

Sculpted ankles, scuffed black Volleys. The mesmerising gulp of his throat as he downs half his schooner.

He wipes his mouth with the back of his wrist and offers his hand.

'Kim.'

Long fingers, calloused palm. Warm but dry.

'Lyssa. I've seen you working in Civic Park.'

Stating the bleeding obvio ...

Cutting Hawkface short, Lyssa flashes, Not one more word, from either of you.

Kim is grinning. 'Yeah. Nice place to eat, under those big old figs. And you? Working or lurking?'

'Working,' she laughs. 'At the Art Gallery. Sort of probation.'

Mutual interest hangs awkwardly in the air. Lyssa bites the bullet.

'Hey, don't you drive that old Kombi with the kayak on top? Do you already know about the Rising Tide protest on Sunday? Blockading the river to stop the coal ships?'

'Yeah, I'll be there for sure. I went out this arvo, to suss out the shipping lane.'

He waits for her to say something. When she doesn't, he hazards, 'You're a paddler?'

'I've done a bit. Lake and sea. I grew up in Forster.'

'Cool. So you've got something to go out in?'

'Not here in Newie. But there'll be a bunch of hired kayaks. I can grab one of those.'

A slow smile turns his brown eyes darker.

'You could jump in with me. If you don't mind sharing with Shanti.'

Momentarily blank, Lyssa asks, 'Your kayak fits three?' Hearing Miz Moon hiss, *It's the bitch, darl*, she corrects herself. 'Oh, Shanti. That's your dog?'

He laughs, 'You saw my dog? So, that *was* you I saw, in the Dog Beach carpark?'

Hawkface splutters, *Good thing it's dark,* as Lyssa feels a blush rising. Deciding the angels are enjoying this way too much, she telegraphs a fierce, *Bugger off!*

Kim is talking about the Art Gallery.

'Sorry?'

'I asked how you landed a job there.'

'It's part time. And temporary. I've worked it into my Masters' degree.'

'Uni, eh?'

Damn. Lyssa waits for irony, something mocking: first rule with Newcastle boys is, don't scare them off with education.

'A Masters. In art?'

She nods,

'Hands on?'

'I sculpt. Casting and welding with bronze, brass, stainless steel, lots of combinations. And I'm researching women's art in public places.'

'You cast bronze? Cool. Tell me more.'

She takes a sip of her beer, unfolds her legs, moves a little closer.

Returning from the bar with two more schooners, Lyssa slides along the bench until her arm touches Kim's.

'So, what were you thinking, out on the river, playing chicken with that coal ship?'

He laughs. 'Playing chicken? Yeah, maybe I was, but it was more about technique.' He gives her a long look. 'Promise to keep this under your hat?'

'Sounds clandestine. What am I promising?'

'Trust me.'

'Okay.'

'Well, back in the 80s, before you were born.'

'Give me a break, I was born in the 80s.'

'This was 1986.'

'A year later,' she concedes.

'Ah, you beat me by a couple.' He looks pleased. 'So, in '86 a protester on a surfboard grabbed hold of the bow of a US nuclear warship as it came into Sydney Harbour.'

Miz Moon whinnies nervously. Lyssa focusses her out. 'Yeah, I've read about him. Proving how effective non-violent protest could be? Seems dangerous on so many levels.'

'Yes and no. Those big ships come in pretty steadily. You just have to be spot-on judging the wave. It was brilliant activism. Worldwide publicity. Mega.'

'So, on Sunday, *you'll* do that in a kayak instead of a surfboard? With your dog? And me?'

'Yeah,' he laughs. 'Could be a bit chancy, I guess. You don't have to.'

Lyssa grins. 'The offer's retracted already? No way! If we can practice tomorrow, I'm totally up for it.'

'Cool.'

Smiling to himself, he starts to draw in a wet glass-ring on the table. Lyssa notices the broken circle inked heavily on his inner wrist.

'Hey, is that a Japanese *ensō*?'

He twists his arm to show her.

'A *yuanxiang*. It was Chinese first. The Japanese nicked it. It's meant to be one fluid stroke, so getting it tattooed was a bit of a contradiction. I drew it up, and I was really happy with how the tattoo artist did it.'

Lyssa traces the shape with one finger, saying softly, 'Chinese? I had no idea.'

She looks up.

'Hey, there's some great street art around town with this tag. Some of it's also signed 'Chi'. So that's you?' *Kim Chi.* Seriously?

He laughs. 'Nice. Few people pick that up.'

His fingers gently circle her wrist.

The bartender has called time and the beer garden is emptying. Lyssa has lost count of the beers. She feels like she's been underwater for the last few hours, oblivious to the music stopping, people talking, glasses being cleared. Headily, she feels for her shoes. Remembering Kim had mentioned earlier that he was studying through TAFE, she says, 'Hey, what's the course you're doing?'

'Oh, yeah. It's an arborist certificate.'

Her sense of intimacy hits a bump.

'An arborist? You're kidding. You want a job killing trees?'

Surprised, he says, 'But tree removal's just a part of the job. There's pruning, lopping, safety issues, disease, assessing habitat like nesting holes. The aim is to keep the trees healthy, not kill them.'

'But now you're working for a Council hellbent on destroying the most beautiful avenue of trees in the city.'

'That's an infrastructure problem,' he says reasonably. 'A good example of what I mean. Roots in drains. Footpath damage. But the Council is hiring experts to assess what can be done. They'll sort it out.'

Out in the street the air is sweet with dope. People linger to talk, laugh, kiss. Lyssa discovers her legs are a little wobbly when she stumbles. Kim's arm shoots out to steady her, and she leans into him. Thinking, Could be a little bit drunk, could be a little bit smitten, she smiles up at him. 'What if they don't?'

'What if who don't what?'

'What if your expert arborists don't 'fix' the Laman Street figs?' What if you get the job to execute those beautiful trees?'

He laughs. 'I don't even have the certificate yet.'

'No! You can't brush this off.'

'Hang on, I'm not.'

Silly doesn't win, Miz Moon moans.

But Lyssa is nettled. Pulling away, she says in an offhand voice, 'Gotta go. My bus-stop's up that way. Tonight has been fun. Thanks, and all that.'

Kim grabs her hand. 'Hey, you're angry? Let's talk about it. And what about our plan, to practice with the kayak tomorrow? Don't go yet.'

Piqued, Lyssa stalls.

'Yet? You mean there's more?'

Her knees almost fold at his smile.

'Could be. The Kombi's just up the road. Let me give you a lift home.'

No guts no glory, Hawkface mutters. For once, Lyssa tells herself, he might be right.

'Maybe,' she teases Kim. 'It depends.'

'Yeah? Depends on what?'

She slides her arms around him and gazes up at his face. 'If the Council did decide to kill the fig trees, would you leave your job?'

'Woah,' he laughs, 'No holding back. It won't happen, believe me, those trees are safe.'

'But would you?' Her voice is silky.

Kim's face is unreadable.

Holding her breath, Lyssa starts to wish, for possibly the first time ever, that the angels had made her stop talking.

But Kim is smiling again. 'For you,' he says, slowly, 'that is distinctly possible.'

Miz Moon squeaks, *Cha cha cha cha bing!*

Wallis Lake, beneath the Forster-Tuncurry bridge, is clear jewelled water. Never flooded. Never muddy. Lyssa, driving her mum's car across for the first time on L plates, asks the cloudy shape beside her, 'Why was I at work with you at the nursing home, Mum? The day I got lost?'

'I was a single mum, darling. If there was no babysitter, management let me bring you in. You were so good. The old people loved you.'

Lyssa turns her head, hoping to see her mother's long hair and beautiful face.

'You found Nige for us,' her mother's voice says, 'weren't we lucky?'

Lyssa heaves a sigh.

'Why are you so hard on him, Lyss?' That constant question.

'He took you away, Mum.'

'Marrying Nige didn't take me away. It brought us Izzy. You love her.' Her mother's voice is sounding echoey.

'But Nige scared me. Mum? Are you leaving? Please stay.'

'It was the other man who scared you, Lyss. Nige saved you. He heard you crying and brought you back to me.' The voice fades away.

'Mum!'

Lyssa is much younger. She is crying for her mother. A man with a pimply face says, 'Mummy went to see the blue flowers. Come with me, I'll take you there.' Taking her hand, he leads her down a track towards a muddy dam. There are blue flowers in the water that look like Thing One and Thing Two from Lyssa's Cat in a Hat book, but she can't see her mum. 'Mummy's in there,' the man says, dragging her towards a tunnel under the road, where cobwebs hang like curtains. Behind them it's dark. Lyssa pulls back, but the man won't let go. Someone else is shouting. The pimply man runs. He slides into the dam. Things One and Two reach for her with their red hands and she shrieks as arms wrap around her.

Lyssa wakes with a gasp in a tangle of sheets and humidity. No matter how often the dream recurs, the release is always shattering. *Childhood trauma.* Psychologists have used that term since before she knew its meaning, but knowing doesn't help. Wishing she'd shut the curtains, she squints through the window-glare. Outside there's a white cockatoo on the clothes hoist. Extending its wings and sulphur crest it shrieks again.

Head pounding, Lyssa shuts her eyes. She slows her breathing and takes herself back to night-safe arms, and mother's whispered mantra: 'Turn the Things back to waterlilies.'

Miz Moon purrs, *Nice work, doll. Atomic sparkler. Big red rocket.*

Lyssa's eyes snap open. Kim!

She rolls over. He is naked beside her, his hair a black fan across the pillow, his skin honeyed by the morning light. Last night at the pub, he mentioned the Chinese grandfather he never knew, a calligrapher who influenced his art. She smiles. That grandfather must have been beautiful.

The Lass O'Gowrie, she muses. Who'd've thought? Drank too much, and here we are.

Body tingling, she tries to piece together everything that happened after they fell together on the bed. At some stage Miz Moon had shrilled, *No way, looney tune.* What was that about, Lyssa wonders. And remembers. She had randomly asked Kim what he thought about angels. He'd stopped flicking his tongue down her belly and she'd frozen, thinking Moon was right. But he was singing words that she didn't recognise. Strangely thrilled, she asked him to sing them again. This time, she heard, 'She says she talks to angels, and they call her out by her name.' 'What's that?' she'd asked, and he'd murmured against her, 'Old favourite, Black Crowes.'

Black Crowes, Lyssa thinks. Need to look them up.

The cockatoo shrieks again.

'Lyss? Are you okay?' Kim's voice is drowsy.

She smiles as she slides down his body. 'Perfectly. Why?'

His fingers ruffle through her hair. 'Must have been dreaming. Thought I heard you scream.'

Horseshoe Beach is alive with flags, banners and milling people, and a cool breeze prinks the river to sparkling. The waves entering at its mouth, corralled by the seawalls and nearly spent, lift the kayak gently as breath. The motion takes Lyssa back to being rocked on a bony lap, the faint smell of pee, and a wavering voice saying, 'My baby, my baby'. Old Maeve, she thinks. She'd be long gone by now. Old Maeve gave me the angels, the day that Nige stopped that guy dragging me away.

The memory will always chill her.

She watches a sea eagle slowly flap across the sky. Wings would have been way more fun, she decides, than angels.

She waits for a response from Miz Moon or Hawkface. Nothing. Not a word from either since yesterday. It feels odd. She's used to them coming and going, but great sex *and* attending a protest? Normally that would be right up their alley.

Picturing her six-year-old self, Lyssa wonders why the angels had stayed. Why hadn't they simply flapped off out of her child-mind?

She feels a wet snuffle at the back of her neck and lifts her arm saying, 'Come on then.'

Shanti pushes past her and stands in the footwell, front paws on the prow, nose to the wind. The dog has happily accepted the extra body in the kayak and spreads her favors equally. Lyssa ruffles her damp coat, crooning, 'Beautiful girl.'

Downstream, the shipping lane is a jumble of canoes, kayaks, rowboats, and rubber duckies, even reckless kids on lilos. There's a yacht with NO MORE COAL painted on its sail and the big Greenpeace catamaran, up from Sydney. A helicopter hovers noisily above the protest pack spread across the middle of the river. Watching the cameraman lean out the side, Lyssa hopes the story will make it to the evening TV news. Not much is happening so far but even without a coal ship coming in they'll have spectacular footage.

A cheer goes up and the chopper heads towards a cumbersome-looking raft, making its way laboriously out from the beach. As it gets closer, Lyssa sees it's made from reclaimed timber and bits of furniture made into a sort of throne. The guy on top pedals as if his life depends on it. And it does, she reminds herself. Newcastle is the world's biggest coal port, and fossil fuels are driving global warming, so it's up to us to stop them exporting all that shit.

She twists to see Kim. 'Looks like hard work. How on earth is he moving that thing?'

'Ah—he's moving it on water.'

He laughs at the look she gives him. 'Paddles at the back. I helped a bit, building it. It's heavy as all fuck, I'd love to know how they got it down to the beach. Reinforces the point, though. Everything out here is powered by wind and muscle.'

'Except for the action support boats. And the Greenpeace cat.'

'A necessary concession.'

'And all the bloody cops burning up fuel and testosterone.'

'Not necessary at all,' Kim grins.

All morning police speedboats and jet skis have zoomed around the protesters like malevolent blue and white wasps. Too many, Lyssa thinks, annoyed at having to abandon yesterday's plan to launch their action from the anonymity of the protest pack. Earlier, when a ship came up the channel, it became clear that the plan had holes in it. Someone on the Greenpeace cat had megaphoned that it was a grain carrier heading for the Carrington silos, and to clear the shipping lane. Despite the protesters beginning to move away, the cops charged around like kelpies on steroids ordering everyone back to shore. They were largely ignored, and the shipping lane reoccupied as soon as the ship went past. But not by Kim and me, Lyssa thinks. Now we have to hang out upriver, and act like casual observers. Which also makes yesterday's practice a little superfluous. Not that we did much practice, we stayed in bed most of the day.

Smiling, she feels her body flood with heat. As if he has read her thoughts, Kim's warm fingers slide over her back and start to knead.

'Hey, Lyss, how're you coping?'

'Even better now.'

Yesterday, she'd claimed the back seat in the kayak for the secret pleasure of watching how his muscles flexed as he paddled. But it was soon obvious that, being the stronger paddler, Kim would need to steer the action. She leans back to the pressure of his hands and tries to let go of the tension that has niggled since they paddled here to the edge of things. Away from the fun. Away from support if something goes wrong.

Blocking that thought, she watches the helicopter head back towards the city. The gothic cathedral, on the hill beyond the CBD, looks down like Batman's head. But the Church hasn't been a defender. More and more reports have emerged about the historic sexual abuse of children by this region's clergy. There's so much that is dark about Newcastle, she decides. Apart from the coal, and ingrained soot from decades of steel production, there's this opaque river, its catchment gouged by mines, its delta islands obliterated for industry, and beyond the environmental, there's a burden of pain that began when the British arrived, inflicted a penal colony in this place, brutalising the convicts and hounding the Awabakal and Wonnarua and Worimi people from their land.

The sea eagle is circling over Nobbys. She imagines flying over the high pointy island before the colonial powers blasted away the top two thirds to change the shipping winds and build the causeway. Nige told Izzy about the Dreamtime kangaroo spirit that lives beneath the island and makes the land shudder when it's angry. Izzy's eyes had widened when he said the big Newcastle earthquake was a sure sign the kangaroo was getting fed up. People dead and buildings reduced to rubble, Lyssa thinks. Another layer of pain. Maybe the kangaroo was objecting to coal mining. And who the hell was Nobby anyway?

Fossicking in her mind for what Nige has called the island, Lyssa pulls the word up and turns its sounds over. *Whibayganba.* We should use that name, she thinks. And Mulubinba for Newcastle. Give them back.

Nige, she sighs. He adored mum and Izzy, but I wouldn't let him near me. Not even at the end, to make mum happy. And Lyssa is back in the stillness of the palliative care ward, her mother's fingers a moth-flutter in her palm, leaning close to hear her breathless, 'He's loved you since the day he found you, Lyss. Never forget.' An hour later she was gone, and Nige had wrapped himself around her and Izzy as if he could stop their world from breaking.

And I didn't resist, she thinks. After all those years of being such a bitch to him, I wanted him to hold me.

Bridges to build. She gives herself a shake.

Kim yells, 'Hey, Robbo!'

Lyssa sees a grey canoe head towards them from the protest pack. She looks back.

'Aren't we meant to be incognito?'

'It's cool. Robbo's a mate. I just need to ask him something.'

The canoe hauls alongside. Shanti wriggles past, tail wagging, and reaches to lick Robbo's hand. Scratching behind her ears, he says gidday to Lyssa and starts to chat about the protest.

Lulled by the sun, Lyssa settles back in her seat. Half-listening, she leans her head on her hand and is lost to the patterns of the river.

She wakes to the sound of shouting. Robbo has moved away and Shanti is nestled back in the well between her feet.

'What's happening?'

'Macho jet-ski cop. Cut through a bunch of the protesters.'

A woman's voice blasts suddenly from the Greenpeace cat. 'Coal ship coming in. Everyone, please hold your places for as long as possible.' Her instructions on strategy and safety awareness are drowned out by the thud of the returning helicopter and the whine of powerboats and jet skis as the police try to herd the protest craft from the shipping lane.

The ship coming in is so big that it seems to take up the river mouth. Watching from the shore, Lyssa has often thought of freighters coming up the river as slow, and somehow majestic. Being up close and personal with the rusting grain carrier that ploughed past earlier in the day had dispelled that illusion. The advancing coal ship looks twice as big and its speed is daunting.

Kim paddles slowly backwards, laughing with excitement. 'Make it look like we're moving,' he calls. 'But don't work too hard, we need to stay in place. Lyss, are you sure you're ready for this?'

'Totally,' Lyssa calls over her shoulder. But, noticing how hard some of the slower protesters downstream have to paddle to get out of the coal ship's way, she doesn't feel so sure.

Something flickers high above the ship's bridge. The sea eagle.

Pinion feathers spread like fingers, it soars low over the ship's prow, heading straight for her. Lyssa gasps and ducks, but not before registering the bird's beaky profile, and the golden globe of its eye like a lens to another world.

The bird swings away, it's harsh *kaakaakaakaakaa* filling her head like a warning.

Kim shouts, 'Now, Lyss. Go hard!'

Lyssa digs in her paddle, vaguely aware of the grey canoe keeping pace like a shadow on one side, as the vast ship looms on the other. She hadn't anticipated this thunder of engines, this cascading roar as the ship gouges the river, that it would be this hard to catch her breath. Stick to the plan, she tells herself nervously, come in obliquely, aim for that gargantuan prow. She feels the kayak lift on the bow wave, but the sheer bulk of the ship is destablilising their trajectory. Kim's cry of exhilaration stalls as the kayak starts to crab sideways.

Shanti slides backwards, her claws scrabbling for purchase. Kim yells. 'Grab her.' As Lyssa lunges for the dog, the kayak cants and tips.

The drag from the ship pulls Lyssa under, her life vest useless. Struggling to find Shanti in the turmoil of currents, she sees instead Miz Moon's face in each bubble that streams upwards. Multitudes of red lips open wide. A chorus of screams shrills in Lyssa's head. Something clamps on her arm. She pictures the pimply man and tries to pull away. Water jets into her nostrils and throat.

Her head breaks into air. Kim's arm is around her chest. Kicking frantically against the ship's drag he says over and over, 'We're okay, Lyss, we're okay.'

She vomits up the river. Struggles for a breath. Vomits again.

The noise and churn of the ship recede.

Kim treads the settling water. Bumping limply against him, Lyssa thinks, call for help, we need help. She feels his body twist. He starts to shout, but is wracked by coughing.

Eyes clenched, Lyssa knows it isn't help that he's looking for, but his dog. She doesn't want to see the empty river, doesn't want to see Kim's frantic face, doesn't want to think about how they've ruined the protest action. She wants the angels, but there is no sense of them anywhere.

She feels the drone of a jet-ski approaching. The sound cuts, and the machine drifts to a careful stop beside them. A deep voice says, 'Good job, bro, keep that hold of her. You can grab onto here, at the side. Yeah, that's it, hang on tight, the support boat's on its way.'

Lyssa opens her eyes to the face of a thick-set young cop. Dark skin, Māori tattoos, big white teeth as he laughs, 'You didn't hear this from me, but that was epic. I'll grab her bro, if you need a rest.'

Don't, Lyssa thinks, don't let me go. Kim's hold stays strong. She hears the rawness of his voice when he asks, 'Can you see a dog anywhere?'

'You took a dog? No way, bro. What were you thinking?'

There is nothing else to say.

The current swings them slowly. Lyssa gazes dully at Horseshoe Beach, the causeway, the lighthouse. The sea eagle is flapping slowly back up-river. Directly below it is a grey canoe. Robbo, paddling hard towards them. He swings alongside. Shanti stands in the seat well behind him, her bedraggled tail wagging.

Only Lyssa feels the rush of air as the sea eagle brushes past. She catches a glimpse of Hawkface before it swings away. The bird climbs on strong wings higher and higher. When it is no more than a speck in the sky, it settles into a slow circle above the river.

11: 2011 Refuge

The doorbell.

'Hang on,'

Tash grabs her stick, levers herself from the couch, and stumps along the hallway. A narrow shape beyond the ripple-glass. She opens the front door to a young woman. Barely twenty, glazed brown eyes, narrow face. White tee, stick thin legs in black jeans. The end few centimetres of her straight black hair bleached dead-white.

Beside her a little girl stares up, her mouth open. Green jumper over a pink tutu, hair like rusty steel wool.

Daughter? Little sister?

The young woman holds up a dirty-orange fluffy toy in cupped hands. 'Is this yours?'

Tash looks down.

Not a toy, a kitten. Head lolling, pale crescent of tongue between needle teeth. Blood oozing through marmalade fur.

The young woman uncurls her fingers to show the kitten's back leg, half-severed. The gleam of bone in raw purple flesh.

'Shit!' Tash steps back. 'Not mine, sorry.'

'But what can we do?' the young woman pleads. 'We've gotta do *something*.'

Tash glances towards her wheelie bin, waiting for collection on the street. 'I'll get you a plastic bag,'

The young woman follows her look. 'Fuck! No! How could you even *think* that?'

'Mumma.'

The child bursts into tears and bunts her mother's leg. Unbalanced, the mother steps sideways. The kitten emits a squeak.

Horrified, Tash says, 'It's alive? Christ! Can't you take it to the vet? The clinic's only two blocks up on Darby.'

The mother, bending to her child, thrusts the kitten at Tash. Who takes it instinctively. Ear-piercing yowl, sticky warmth.

The mother pulls the little girl onto her hip and backs away, her voice harsh over the child's wails. 'I can't. I've got no money. Sorry, but I just can't fucking *do* this.'

She turns abruptly and her hair swings back. The side of her face looks red, swollen.

Stunned, Tash watches them rush out the gate, the child yelling '*I want the kitty*', arms and legs thrashing.

A few metres on, the mother puts her daughter down. Through the fence-wire Tash sees the child thump on her bottom. She screams while the mother picks up a crumpled backpack and shoves in what's scattered over the footpath. A water bottle, pencils, pieces of fruit. She slings the pack over her shoulder, hoists the sobbing child in her arms, checks the street in both directions, and hurries off towards the park.

Tash closes the door and walks back to the kitchen with the kitten clutched to her stomach. No sound from it now, but a shudder with each small breath.

Pulling tea-towels from a drawer, she swaddles it carefully and nests it in the bottom of her shopping trolley. She grimaces at each hollow thump of her walking stick on the timber floor as she makes her way back along the silent hallway.

The far window table is free in Natural Tucker's cramped café space.

'Sorry, 'scuse me, sorry,' Tash says, bumping between the other tables to bags it with her library satchel. She repeats the performance as she returns to order at the counter. On her third pass a guy in a leather jacket mutters to his companion as he makes an exaggerated effort to move his chair one centimetre to let her through. Tash hears *fat* and *clumsy*. She refrains from thumping him with her stick, hooks it over the spare chair at her table and settles. Judgemental twat. And too bad about the clumsy, everyone knows space is tight here, so suck it up.

She smiles gratefully when the barista brings over her coffee instead of calling her name, the glorious wave of tangerine above his dark undercut making her regret her own hair's fading crimson and white zebra stripe of roots.

'Great 'do', Geordie.'

Geordie grins, 'Glad you like it.'

Pulling *The Girl Who Kicked the Hornet's Nest* from her satchel, Tash opens it at the bookmark. Absorbed in Lisbeth Salander's precarious hold on life, she doesn't look up until a shrill voice demands, 'Chockie milk, Mumma. *Chockie*.'

The mother and child from a while back, the little girl's pink fairy wings strapped crookedly over a black and yellow-striped top, her rusty hair restrained in two high bunches. The mother's hair looks lank, the bleached ends dull. Tash wonders if the bruise still shows on her cheek.

The child dances eagerly as the mother pulls a bottle from the drinks' fridge. She wails 'No, Mumma, *Chockie*' when she realises it's apple juice. Geordie's face lights up at the sight of them. He turns in profile and slicks a hand theatrically over his bright hair before offering a banana over the counter.

'Nana! Open it for me, Mumma.'

The mother goes through her purse as she chats with Geordie. Handing the peel back with the coins, she turns for the door. Seeing Tash, she hesitates.

Tash wants to call out, point to the spare seat at her table, but leather jacket guy is leaning back in his chair as if he owns the place. Through the window, she sees the mother check out both directions of Darby Street as if making up her mind. She turns right and the child trots after her, banana clasped in grubby hands, wings wobbling.

Not much of a fairy, Tash thinks.

Turning the corner out of Bull Street into Bruce, Tash sees them up ahead. Outside her house. The mother's hands are jammed on her hips and the child clings to the buttress of the fig tree on the nature strip, shrieking, 'No, *no*.'

Noticing Tash, the child lets go and bolts towards her, yelling, 'Kitty. I wanna see the kitty.' She spins back to her mother: 'Mumma, the *kitty*. I wanna see it.'

'Bee! Get back here.'

The mother grabs the child by the shoulder and looks along the street behind Tash before saying, 'Hi. Yeah. Sorry. About the kitten.'

The child tries to wriggle away. Grasping her wrist, the mother says in a rush, 'Bee's driving me nuts, obsessing about that kitten. Every bloody day it's been *take me back, I want to go back.* What can you tell them?' She raises her voice over the child's whingeing. 'I felt like crap, you know, dumping it on you. We were in a bad place.'

'Kitty, kitty, *kitty*.' The child buckles at the knees.

'Listen kid,' Tash says firmly. 'Stop yelling about the kitten. It's okay.'

Hopeful silence. The mother looks confused. 'But it's dead, yeah?'

Tash leans over her stick to open her gate. 'Come in and see.'

The kitten is already transforming to cat. Orange fur conceals most of the scar on its hip as it races three-legged along the back of the couch. It crouches, leaps out of sight, and reappears dragging a tangle of turquoise string.

Delighted, Bee squeals, 'What's her name? What's her name?'

'He's called Pushkin,'

'Pusska!' Bee runs to grab the string.

Tash had introduced herself in the hallway as Bee raced ahead. The mother said her name was Mishell, and spelled it, adding 'But I prefer Mikki now.' They watch child and kitten tussle. Tash asks, 'Bea? Short for Beatrice?

'It's just Bee. Two 'e's. Her father named her Bailee. I changed it.'

The child picks up on the conversation and begins to buzz. Arms wide she circles the kitten, yelling, 'I'm Bee, Pusska. Busy buzzy Bee'.

Tash offers tea.

'Sure, thanks.'

'Reali-tea or herbal?'

Mikki laughed.

'Peppermint, if you've got it.'

Tash puts the kettle on. Bee, collapsed to her knees on the floor, nurses the kitten like a baby. Mikki wanders around the living room.

'Nice place.'

'Thanks.'

'Can't believe how much space you've got. Looks small from the street.'

'I had this part built on. I need the room. Because of the stick.'

Mikki cups her hand around a protea in the tall vase on the dining table. Tash resists the urge to explain that she only managed to afford the extension because of the compo from a work accident. Dragging her claim through courts and being torn to shreds by lawyers was a lesson in the value of not offering information unless asked.

Mikki pulls a book from the bookshelf, reads both covers, puts it back and picks up a framed photo. She reads aloud, 'Natasha Jales, First Year Fitting and Machining Apprentice Award, 1988, BHP Steelworks, Newcastle.'

'Wow! This is you?'

Tash looks up from filling the mugs. It's the photo taken for an article on Affirmative Action in the Herald. Tanned, lean and muscled, wearing a hard hat and sleeveless overalls that showed the workplace logo, she'd held up her award certificate with a proud smile. The boiling water spills. Swearing under her breath she reaches for a cloth. Go on girl, do the bloody maths, she thinks bitterly. Twenty-three years ago, and here I am well in my forties with nothing to show.

Mikki swings around. 'You looked ripped back then, hey.' Her grin vanishes when she sees Tash's face.

'Sorry. Shouldn't have said that.'

Why the fuck not, Tash thinks, throwing the cloth in the sink. Why not just say I look a lot bloody older? It's the truth.

Mikki bends to tickle Bee, slumped on the couch with Pushkin asleep on her chest. Bee giggles. Tash offers a glass of milk. The child shakes her head sleepily.

The women sip their tea in awkward silence at the dining table, Mikki, taking in the glossy pot-plants beside the open glass doors, the greenness bordering the bricked terrace. Eventually she asks, 'Do you do all that yourself? Like those plants and stuff?'

Tash nods.

'I'd like to grow things. Keep them healthy-looking like that.'

Envy edging her voice.

Tash says brusquely, 'Look, I've never been a cat person. I only agreed to keep him because the vet offered to fix him for free if I did. You and Bee rescued him, why don't you take him home?

'No way!' Mikki's voice hard.

'Why not? Bee seems pretty attached.'

Quietly, fiercely, Mikki says, 'Because we live at the fucking refuge. And we're the reason that kitten got hurt in the first place. He was wandering in the street and Bee was playing with him, then her father ... He's a bastard, he tracks us.'

'Mumma?

'Fuck!'

Mikki buries her face in her hands. After a moment she gets up, goes to her daughter and leans to take the kitten. Bee clutches it, saying anxiously, '*No*, Mumma, I want Pusska.' Mikki lifts them both onto her hip and returns to the table. She finishes her tea standing, talking in a bright, hard, distracting voice about a thrush scratching in the garden.

At the front door Tash says to the child still clinging to the uncomplaining kitten, 'You have to give him back to me now, hon.'

Bee offers the kitten up, saying 'Goodbye Pusska.' She grabs Tash's arm in a tight little hug.

'Good girl.' Mikki looks shyly at Tash. 'You take care of your plants real well. You should look after yourself like that.'

'What?'

'You looked great in that photo. Short hair suited you. You shouldn't let your roots get that grey. I can fix them for you. You know, a cut, new dye.'

'You're a hairdresser?'

'Yeah, I wish.' Her voice flat as she turns away.

'Well, nothing to lose, I guess. If you think you can do a good job.'

Mikki swings back. 'I've got proper scissors and stuff. I've done plenty of girlfriends. And that guy at Natural Tucker? I did him. I'm pretty good.'

'Sounds like a plan. When can you do it?'

'I'll have to buy the dye and stuff,' Mikki says. 'And I don't have the money.'

Bee pulls a pinecone tied to a piece of string around the courtyard, her squeals each time Pusska pounces shrill even through closed doors. The glass is smeared with Bee-height hand marks. Tash smiles. There's a trail of chaos each time the kid comes over. But even cleaning up when she's gone is something of a pleasure.

This is the third time she has minded Bee. The first, a doctor's appointment, saw Mikki rush back within an hour with the panicked expression of a mother who'd trusted her child to someone she hardly knew. She had laughed with relief when Bee grizzled that she didn't want to leave. The second, a dreaded mediation session with the child's father, took up a whole morning. This time Mikki had called at midday to say she had a three o'clock appointment with her caseworker, Jazz, to check out a subsidised share-house in New Lambton and would Tash mind? 'Shouldn't be more than two hours,' she'd said, dropping Bee off. 'I'd take her with me but she's been ratty all day and she'll do my head in with questions while I'm trying to think.'

It is almost time for the six o'clock news. Would a house inspection take this long, Tash wonders. Maybe the house offer came good and there's a pile of paperwork to fill? Maybe Mikki and the caseworker are indulging in a celebration chardy?

She starts to look for her phone. No doubt Bee's been playing with it again. Glancing at the living-room mirror as she passes, she moves close to check her roots.

Still fine after nearly a fortnight. Mikki did a good job. The colour's redder than Tash expected but the cut looks great, more like her old style. Handing over that fifty bucks, she'd half-expected it would be the last she'd see of Mikki. But she'd come back, with the products and the change. They'd set up in the kitchen to keep an eye on Bee, tearing around the house and courtyard. Mikki washed Tash's hair at the sink and massaged in a treatment, and after Bee was fed and settled with Pusska in front of the TV, she'd carefully cut, dyed, styled and dried.

Afterwards, she'd taken Tash to this mirror, to show off the result, and Tash had joked, 'Maybe you should move in, become my private hairdresser.' But Mikki didn't laugh, she didn't say anything, and Tash had let the moment pass.

Why shouldn't they move in here, Tash thinks, discovering her phone and the TV remote under a couch cushion. I like their company.

I have the room. Who knows, it could work. Maybe I'll suggest it when Mikki gets back.

She turns the set on ready for the NBN news and mutes it to call Mikki. The phone rings out twice. The News coverage starts of the Melbourne Cup. Leaving it muted, Tash goes to check what Bee is doing in the courtyard. The child, ensconced in the shaded butterfly chair, has taken off her frilly yellow top and wrapped Pusska in it. The cat stares up passively at his captor's face.

Tash calls from the door, 'Hungry, hon? Want an apple?'

'Samwich. Honey samwich. Peanut butter too.' Bee starts to climb out of the chair.

'Stay there, in the shade. I'll bring it out. A little picnic.'

'A picnic!' The child claps her hands in delight.

Tash flicks up the volume on the remote, returns to the kitchen and props her stick beside the fridge, half-watching the posturing punters, ejaculating champagne bottles, ridiculous hats, betting tickets and other litter trodden into the grass. The reporter's excited voice-over announces, 'Dunaden won by a cat's whisker'. Horse's whisker more like it, Tash grins. She mashes peanut butter and honey together on a slice of bread to news of the world population reaching seven billion and another boatload of asylum seekers sinking off Indonesia.

The newsreader's voice drops a register. 'To local news now and a report just to hand, this afternoon two women were taken by ambulance to John Hunter Hospital, after a vicious attack in New Lambton. Police have taken a man into custody.'

Tash drops the sticky knife on the floor as she swings to look out the kitchen window. '... a Women's Refuge case worker discharged soon after,' she hears, '... twenty-two-year-old client remains in intensive care with severe head injuries.'

Out in the butterfly chair Bee intently probes a scab on her knee. Leaf shadows move over her bare shoulders. Pusska is nowhere to be seen. 'Police are calling for assistance in locating the younger woman's four-year-old daughter,' the newsreader is saying. 'The arrested man is believed to be the child's father.'

Tash grabs her stick. She needs to scoop Bee up, cocoon her.

Passing the living room mirror, Tash stops in her tracks and stares. Her hair looks as red as blood. Leaning heavily on her stick, she wills herself back from that image. Back in time. Back to Mikki and Bee's giggles as they'd cuddled goodbye. Back to the disbelief on Mikki's face when Tash first offered to babysit.

To how Mikki constantly looked behind.

To each moment Tash could have offered refuge.

She wants the white zebra-stripe to still be in her fading crimson hair.

She wants to open her front door to a young woman with a child and a nearly dead kitten, and to instantly understand.

12: 2012 Trees for Life

His name is Garrett. The woman who left him all those years ago, taking their little girl Amber, was Sherry.

He had been a buff young bloke, stringy muscles, never far from a surf. Girls liked him but it was Sherry, with her dark upswept brows, halo of honey-gold hair and skin tanned to the colour of her name, who loved him. When they first had sex, on damp sand beneath an overhang at Caves Beach, she told him he was perfect.

Four months later his number came up in the conscription draft. The day before he began military training, Sherry used clippers to cut off his surfer locks. She ran her hand over his prickly scalp with an uncertain laugh.

He'd been only a couple of months in Vietnam when he read Sherry's letter telling him she was pregnant. The following day, on patrol, the warm dream that news had wrapped him in was shredded by a land mine. The army doctors decided that with so much flesh and muscle missing from his thigh and calf, amputation was the only option. But swayed by his pleading, they primed him with drugs, packed his leg in ice and put him on a military flight back to Australia. After months of steel rods, skin grafts and rehab he left the hospital on both his legs. He never wore shorts again.

At least he was home when Amber was born.

They got hitched once he could manage without crutches. He was twenty-one, and Sherry eighteen. The wedding photos, taken beneath the spreading fig trees above Newcastle's Civic Park, didn't show the pain of standing. At the reception, in the backyard of Sherry's family home in Cooks Hill, her dad took him aside to say, 'It won't be easy on you son, but you have to promise to look after her. Be the man she's bargaining on.'

With his army severance pay, they bought a dirt-cheap block with a small cabin at the far end of Sunrise Road, west of Dora Creek. Eight steep scrubby acres with a narrow-gutted view east to Lake Macquarie and no near neighbours. But one day there would be. His first job was planting quick-growing natives around the perimeter. Banksias, grevilleas, melaleucas, callistemons. For the birds, he told Sherry. She helped as much as she could on the renovations and was a dab hand with the paintbrush. But she had the baby to care for, so it was pretty much up to him.

That first summer in the cabin was a scorcher. He'd get home from his part-time job detailing cars and work until dark, building a wide verandah. For the shade, and to keep his daughter safe. He mightn't have been a hands-on dad but showed he cared in other ways. He finished the gate across the stairs at dusk on a Sunday and took a cold shower while Sherry peeled potatoes at the sink, watching through the open window as Amber explored her new domain. Sarong slung around his hips, he grabbed a beer from the fridge and wandered back out to roll a joint. Hot air prickled his wet skin as he stepped around his daughter who tractored on all fours, chubby legs propping her nappy-clad bottom high. He sank into a canvas director's chair, scrunched the sarong around his thighs to catch the faint breeze, and ripped the tab off the VB.

The instant relief of icy ale.

Amber pulled herself to her feet against the outside table and turned to appraise him. Tendrils of red-gold hair stuck to her damp cheeks.

With a toothy grin she released her grip and staggered half a dozen steps towards him, saving herself, as her legs collapsed, by flinging her arms around his calf.

At his shout, Sherry rushed out and scooped Amber up, away from the gordian knots of his skin. Sherry crying. But not with joy over her daughter's first steps.

Trembling and wordless, he stood up, went inside and pulled on a pair of jeans.

That night he dreamed he couldn't stop his daughter's limbs from dissolving.

Sherry didn't leave him because of violence. That was the rumour, because he was a Vietnam Vet. She never said it, but he knew it was his leg. Beside him for all the operations and months of rehab, she never asked what happened and after the bandages came off, she never touched the scars. Not once. Not even in that dreamy, otherish way she once used to stroke him with the back of her hand, as if absorbing another dimension of him through her soft, thin skin. In bed she flinched if she felt the mess of gristle and overstrung muscle against her. The one time he tried to talk about it, her body stiffened. 'Don't,' she'd said. 'Don't tell me. I just can't.'

Slowly he removed himself. To the far side of the bed. From the couch they shared to a lounge chair. He spent more and more sullen hours in his shed or working on the block. He smoked joints for the pain and was known as the local stoner.

One evening, he arrived home to a house tidier than it had ever been, neat as a needle through his heart. The same words were written in the neat childish hand of her note: 'It's not you, I just can't. I'm going back to my parents. You can visit, stay part of Amber's life.'

Can't what, he wondered numbly. Cope with the cut-off place he'd brought her to? The stoned, sullen man he'd become? His shame?

And how could he face Sherry's father when he'd failed so completely at being the man she'd bargained on?

In the blank years after Sherry and Amber left, construction of the Eraring coal-fired power station started to consume the view of the lake, and signs of early balding became alopecia.

Stress, his doc said.

It was hard not to feel blighted.

A few years of government-funded wound-picking ended with his counsellor telling him two things: focus on his strengths instead of his failings, and get out among other people.

He bought himself an early Christmas present—the only one as it turned out—a ticket to the Midnight Oil gig in Speers Point Park.

It was 1984 and he was thirty-two.

At the gig, when people stared, he turned away like a worm retracting from light. The eyebrows were the worst of it. Every other bald man had them except, he saw, when Midnight Oil slammed onto the stage, the Oils' front man, Peter Garrett. He didn't share the singer's string-bean leanness and gaunt sculpted face, but they had height and hairlessness in common.

The band pounded into its first set as the day faded to dark. Manic colours lit up the stage. Anonymous in the crowd, he drew back on a joint and relaxed, buoyed by the grinding power of the music and the spectacle of the technicolour sweat flung from Peter Garrett's gyrating body. Until a moment midway through *Short Memory*, when a red stage-spot lit the singer's dancing skull like fire.

Overwhelmed by the remembered stench of burning flesh, it took all the self-talk he could muster to stop himself bolting.

Staying felt like victory.

At the end of the gig, under the glare of floodlights, he found himself mock-punched and back-slapped by departing fans who laughingly hailed him with variations of 'Garrett! Heeeey, Garrett!' He started to smile.

That night at Speers Point, he left behind the names that had pulled him through childhood, war, marriage and becoming a father, and took on a new one.

It was after the Oils concert that Garrett began to plant his forest. The first nineteen trees were dedicated to the Hunter Valley soldiers killed in the Vietnam War. He burnt the names with a soldering iron on timber tags he hung on each seedling. The twentieth, a native frangipani that would one day scent the evening air with musk, he named Kim Phuc for the child whose image, snatched out of time by a photographer, had seared into the consciousness of millions back in '72. A nine-year-old running naked along a broken road, her clothes burnt off by napalm, the skin of her torso and out-flung arms peeling in slabs.

That child at least had a name.

And using her name helped mask the horror of the day two small Vietnamese children had smiled shyly at his greeting of *chào em* as they stepped aside on a jungle track to let him pass. A second later he was sprawled in the mud with the stink of burnt flesh in his throat, his jungle greens gone and parts of his leg dangling like meat on a butcher's hook. The first sound in the ringing silence was his own scream when, pushing himself up to look for the children, he saw the boy's severed head, eyes and mouth wide-open.

Eventually five hundred and twenty-two mulched and vigorous young native trees surrounded the cabin, their common, botanical, and memorial names noted on a carefully drawn map. All but one represented an Australian who died in the conflict, none of whom Garrett knew personally.

When he couldn't sleep, he would grab a torch and wander out and talk to them. He spent a winter's night with a bottle of bourbon and several spliffs rambling to the slender brushbox he'd nicknamed Smithy. Every so often he angled the torch beam up at the leaves, to check the tree was listening.

The native frangipani was the tree he talked to most.

Sherry moved to Forster and found another man for Amber to call Dad. When Garrett drove up to take his five-year old out for a day, she hid behind her mother.

The divorce went through. Sherry didn't make a claim on the Dora Creek block.

Over the next fifteen years Garrett got his benders under control, supplementing his unemployment benefit with handyman jobs and the occasional dope crop. He paid what child maintenance he could and convinced himself that Amber was better off without him. His monologues with the trees dwindled, but he sometimes found himself telling the native frangipani things a father might say to a growing daughter. Deep down, he hoped she would make contact when she was older.

When Amber was eighteen, Garrett discovered she'd had a baby. He had driven north to Tuncurry to buy a second-hand trailer. Waiting in a fast-food shop for a slow burger, he flipped through the local newspaper and was stopped by a half-glance at the New Arrivals column. He knew his daughter's face before he read the caption. The baby girl wrapped tightly in her arms wasn't named, but she was noted as a first grandchild for Sherry and the bloke who gave her and Amber a different surname.

There was no mention of Garrett.

Staring at the photo, he'd muttered 'You could have found me.' But he knew it wasn't up to Amber. He had relinquished being her father. He felt like he didn't exist.

By 2010, when news came through of Newcastle Council's plans to remove the fig trees above Civic Park, Garrett looked as gaunt as his namesake. The destruction of mature trees in a shade-starved city was beyond his comprehension and saving them became an urge he didn't question.

Ficus microcarpa var. hillii. Hill's weeping figs. They were magnificent.

One evening, lying with other protesters on the bitumen of Laman Street, meditating for the tree's survival with small hard fig-balls pressing into his back—something which would previously have been well beyond his comfort zone—he had an out-of-body experience. The city noises began to recede and his body seemed to rise through the arching grey branches until he floated in pure chlorophyll light in the canopy. The woman next to him began to cry with big gulping sobs.

The meditation ended and Garrett clambered to his feet. The woman, who wore her greying plaits looped around her head and layered clothes that were mostly purple, looked about his age. She was wiping her face with the heel of her palms.

Garrett extended his hand.

She shook her head and heaved herself up, saying with a damp smile, 'Sorry. I hope I didn't spoil it for you.'

'Don't worry, you didn't.'

He watched her take in the avenue of arching foliage. 'I was married under these trees. Divorced now, but that's not the point. Bloody Newcastle Council doesn't give a rat's arse.'

Garrett liked her frankness but resisted the impulse to say his story was similar. He watched her walk off towards Darby Street and wondered at his own compulsion to protect the trees. Above him, the tracery of leaves and limbs was black against a teal sky. He thought of the wedding photos taken beneath them, nearly forty years ago. It occurred to him that he had never joined a Veterans' group, or marched on Anzac Day, dismissing the commemoration named for the country's biggest military defeat as glorifying war. Yet he had planted a forest to honour dead soldiers he'd never met, and now he was fighting for the lives of these figs.

His marriage felt like his own biggest defeat. But didn't Amber and her mother also deserve to be honoured?

On the day the first fig tree was to be felled, Garrett reached Laman Street before dawn. Early enough to take part in breaching the fencing before the dozy security guys twigged. Some protesters scrambled into the trees. Garret, less agile, looped the chain he'd brought through a hole in a buttress root, wrapped it around himself and snapped the padlock shut.

Seated on the ground against the buttress, half-registering snatches of conversation around him, he heard his name. He glanced up at the two shapes silhouetted in the tree above him.

'C'mon, seriously,' the boy was muttering. 'Just Garrett? Who else goes by one name? Dealers? Nutters? Bats in the garret if you ask me.'

'I didn't ask you', the girl said softly. 'And it's *belfry*, dickbrain. The term is bats in the *belfry*.'

Garrett smiled, recognising the voice of Lyssa, a lean young woman with cropped white-bleached hair and dark upswept eyebrows who had chatted with him at previous protests. Her muffled laugh was the sound of someone sure of love and the language of teasing. In the early days, Sherry had laughed like that when he murmured against her warm skin, 'I'm going to drink you down to the last sweet drop.'

A few weeks back, Lyssa had told him earnestly that figs held the power to save themselves. 'Figs are the only tree to flower inside their own fruit,' she'd said. 'The flowers are fertilised when tiny wasps tunnel in to lay their eggs. Isn't that the ultimate form of protection?'

The sun rose and more protesters arrived. Security guards, standing with spread legs and crossed arms in front of the roughly reinstated barricade, began to shift nervously as the crowd thickened. Demands of Save Our Trees turned into a chant. Police in riot gear arrived and thrust through the protesters, pushing some to the ground. The chant changed to 'Shame. Shame.'

Garrett had been nervous at the prospect of arrest but beyond a little rough handling by the officer using the bolt cutters it was no big deal. The applause as he was frog-marched towards the police vans made him feel he'd achieved something.

He was loaded into the same paddy wagon as Lyssa, whose boyfriend had already been dispatched in an earlier van. Sitting opposite each other, they watched through the rear window as men wearing hi-vis, hardhats and earmuffs arrived, chainsaws held like weapons. Garrett turned to say something to Lyssa and found her gazing at him. She looked away as if caught out, and said bleakly, 'I always thought an arborist's job was to save trees.'

At the Police Station Lyssa asked an officer about where her boyfriend would be and was told to join the line of protesters being processed. She flashed Garrett a grin when he gestured for her to go ahead of him. Standing behind her, he noticed the roots of her bleached hair were the colour of honey, almost amber. He thought again of Sherry and unconsciously reefed up his track pants, twitched his flannel shirt straight.

Garrett expected Lyssa to bolt in search of the boyfriend when her processing was done but she lingered, waiting. He stepped up to the desk to give his details, the sound of his real name forming an unfamiliar shape in his mouth.

Walking out, Lyssa said 'So you live at Dora Creek?'

'Yep.'

'Funny, I'm sure I haven't been there, but Sunrise Road? I know I've heard that before. Would you ...?' She laughed self-consciously, 'No, forget it. Too weird.'

'What's weird?'

At that moment Garrett heard a shout.

'Lyss!'

Beyond the sliding glass doors, the boyfriend was waving his arms. Lyssa shouted 'Kim'. She did a little spin as she danced towards him. He reached for her and pulled her close.

Garrett wandered to the curb and waited for a gap between the passing cars. The day was cool, but he felt sweaty. Hunching from the breeze to light a cigarette, he looked back. Lyssa and the boy, long black hair bunched on top of his head, were talking intently, faces close.

'Hello! They nabbed you, too?'

It was the woman from the meditation, wearing blues and greens this time. She held the arm of a younger man.

'Did you hear about the injunction? The Land and Environment Court has stopped the chop. My son heard on the car radio coming to pick me up. A week's grace! We could save the trees yet. Do you need a lift back to Civic?'

Smiling, Garrett said he needed the walk.

He watched them stroll down Watt Street before looking back at Lyssa. Still talking, she slowly stroked the back of her hand down her boyfriend's cheek. He took a last drag on his fag, squashed the tip and dropped it in the gutter. About to step into the gap after a battered Mercedes passed by, he heard Lyssa shout his name and swung around. Grinning broadly, she gave him the thumbs up and yelled, 'Nice work'.

He waved and turned away.

On the day the last fig tree was cut to the ground, Garrett drove home to Dora Creek with an ache in his chest and his mind choked with images of severed limbs.

It was one week into February. By evening the heat in the cabin was oppressive. His sarong slung around his hips, he slumped to the couch to watch the local news. Over the whine of chainsaws and footage of an amputated branch crashing to the street the newsreader announced, 'Seventy years sees the end of an era for the Laman Street figs.' The camera panned over screaming protesters and zoomed in on a bald, red-faced old man with a gaping hole where his words should have been.

Garrett recognised himself. His roar filled the empty shack.

Unable to watch more, he went out to the verandah. Lyssa hadn't turned up to the protest that morning. Perhaps he would never see her again. He pictured her upswept brows and imagined her hair unbleached. Her face so familiar. She'd heard of Sunrise Road. Something a grandmother might mention?

The hot westerly wind carried a whiff of bushfire. So far, his summer had been taken up with protests, leaving little time to protect his own trees.

He grabbed his smokes and lighter, shoved his feet into an old pair of Crocs and limped down the steps to get a rake from the shed.

The identification tags in the forest were long gone, but Garrett mentally greeted each tree by name as he passed. He stopped at the native frangipani to cache his fags and lighter in a pinch between trunk and branch. Overshadowed, it had grown tall and spindly. He hadn't seen it flower in years.

He began to rake at the top of his block, the vulnerable western boundary. The sky faded from blue to pink to pale green as he heaped dry grass and leaves, and piled fallen branches on top. Sweat streamed from his face and armpits, down the furrow of his back. The sarong slid from his hips. He left it on the ground.

The wind eased and the air was honeyed by flowering bloodwoods.

By the time he had raked down to the native frangipani, he was gasping for breath. He fumbled in the dimness for his cigarettes, lit up and coughed as smoke filled his lungs. Chest heaving, he stared at the distant power station. It had polluted the region for decades and taken over his lake view but now, as the sky behind it began to glow gold, the lights and twin smokestacks looked ethereal.

The moon. One night past full but still huge. He felt the earth turn towards it.

Hearing the harsh growl of a nearby koala, his mind segued to the snarl of chainsaws, the crash of falling limbs, shattered children. He remembered Amber's perfect little body. The joy on Sherry's face the day she was born.

Why didn't I fight to save my marriage, he wondered. I've never saved anything.

Pain exploded in his chest.

His knees concertinaed and the cigarette arced from his fingers as he thudded to the unraked ground. He watched the bright red tip roll erratically down the slope. It dimmed. Seemed to extinguish.

Unable to move, Garrett stared at the lights of his neighbours' houses below. Cars hummed on the main road. The sound changed. A car was slowing. Garrett saw the headlights swing. He could hear the spit of gravel as it came slowly along Sunrise Road.

A flame was flickering where the cigarette had landed. It licked delicately up the slope towards him.

The car veered into his driveway. Doors slammed. He heard Lyssa call, 'Garrett? Garrett are you here?'

Garrett found his voice.

'Up here, on the hill,' he roared. 'Help! *Help me.*'

Coda: Not YET

There was totally NO CHANCE of finding somewhere after Dozzy's place FLOODED even though People had been saying for years about Melting Ice and the shitStorms getting wilder and stuff but it's easy to think not YET so hardly anybody made preparations some couldn't others wouldn't and every single one of us who lived in the Low Areas like Carrington when the sea started crashing through to the rooftops had to end up looking for Shelter. But lots didn't find.

But Dozzy GOT LUCKY getting the Signal Box at Hamilton station to live in Straight Up before anyone else thought it though maybe it wasn't luck maybe she asked one of her LovelyMen to make that happen because some of them are pretty IMPORTANT she's got a List going back years and I also got lucky because she said I could still SHARE like she's done for years and years now since my brain was cracked. The sign she got made to hang outside says Signal BOX, *Dozzy & Mikki,* because she says it's my place too.

The Signal BOX is really really small which doesn't matter because we've got UpstairsDownstairs like that old tv show way way back. Dozzy's Up even though stairs are hard for her now but she says she likes to be On Top which is TRUE when I'm outside on the DayStreet I see her sitting at her window watching the kids paddle their plastic tubs and little rafts where Styx Creek swelled into a lake over the old shunting tracks between Fern Street and Hudson and if there's been another big sStorm People'll be out looking for UsefulStuff like food or pans or even furniture and bits of wood to fix things with from whatever has washed through. The Signal BOX didn't need much fixing though its made of real bricks and the railways looked after their places built the tracks and everything up high in case of RainFloods but they never thought way back then about Ice Shelves Collapsing and SeaFloods washing whole sections away

But we are SNUG

and Dozzy got tiny bathrooms built for her and me that I clean out for us every day and a little KITCHEN in My Part Downstairs where I can bake and before I go out to the NightStreets with my Backpack of Helpful Things for the GiRLs I make dinner for Dozzy and take it Up

unless she's got a LovelyMan with her

What's good about being On The Bottom is I can peek through the curtain to keep an eye when one of them goes up the Stairs and after he leaves I can check if she needs anything. I like to look out for Dozzy she's looked out for me ever since I was not long OUT OF HOSPITAL and I used to walk around town and when I was sitting on a bench outside Civic Station People turned up with their Signs saying Keep The Trains In Newcastle and some stared because my head was still in bandages. But not Dozzy she was Dolly then and dressed pink all over spiky shoes long glitter dress hot pink hair teased up so beautiful and she came over and asked if I would help her hold up a banner so I did and she told me that Council was planning to take the Heart out of The City so Developers Could Profit and when I told her I was living in The Refuge and people from Community Services had taken daughter she said Why Don't You Stay With Me For A While. In the end all the protests didn't work the rail line got ripped up and the nice old stations at Wickham and Civic and Newcastle were left empty and instead we got the Stupid Tram but I got Dozzy for my friend. She says its Ir-onic that where they put The Interchange is flooded now so the tram is useless anyway and It's Not Like We Weren't All Warned.

Dozzy's done Upstairs really nice deep red walls and pink lights all plush Obvious But Inviting Like Me she says so I laugh Dozzy IS Inviting not beautiful no you wouldn't think she doesn't have that sort of face and she's short and round but she's GLAM she used to be famous still has the wigs and gowns from when she was *Dolly Devine* and did all The Shows back in the Nineties and Naughties but even though she's old now it's hard to tell because she knows Every Trick In The Looks Book. Sometimes I watch her put on her make up SPACKLE she calls it for Filling The Cracks and it does cover up That's The Art Of The Drag Queen she says not that she calls herself that now

Since She Had Her *OP*.

A lot of People must've been sad when she stopped being Dolly Devine. Dozzy says her singing was Rubbish but her Lip-Sinc was

PERFECT and she would Crack Everyone Up when she introduced herself as an *Artiste Of The Lips*. She's always telling me It's Not About Looks and never has been because we are all Beautiful In Our Own Way and You Are Proof Of That MikkiLove And It's More Important To Be Kind. Dozzy's kind and I think that's why her LovelyMen keep Coming. Some of them knew her right back when she was Dolly and she has a fat little book full of their names and things she knows about them and there are others who used to work with the Railways and come to the Signal BOX because They Still Like To Press Levers And Buttons and Dozzy winks when she says that so I laugh though I didn't laugh I got anxious when she said A RailwayMan One Wants To Move In So He Can Play All The Time but then she said Don't Worry MikkiLove I'll Always Say NO.

I like living at the Hamilton End of The Strip it feels safer with more GiRLs about on the NightStreets and more Regular People too when there are still some Shops or a Pub open I get spooked down the Islington end with all those empty Car Yards and the old Fig Trees in the Park dead because Sea Water's drowned their giant roots and I always have to look out for The Roaches which is what People call the NightRoamer gangs that steal and deal and sometimes hurt. Though I don't mind The Wraiths. They are also NightRoamers but they go out in little groups to scavenge what's left of drowned Buildings and keep out of other people's business. I liked Hamilton best though when The Trains used to come through they were company at Night with the Crossing Lights flashing red-red and I always knew if the moan of The Hooters sounded longer and The Rail's clicketty clacking was louder then Rain Was On Its Way. Not that I don't hear hooting and moaning here most Nights when I get home. Dozzy says when a LovelyMan's chugging away it's like A Train Going Through and she provides The Siren. That's funny. But sometimes there's a ManSiren too that's deep and scary like Tugs and Big Ships out on The River or like a person moaning on the footpath with their Head Cracked and Blood Everywhere. Which Was Me so I turn the radio up. It doesn't seem right hearing Private Business. Some of them like what Dozzy calls her A-cout-re-ments and one brings his own Little Black Suitcase like you'd take to the Office with a Whip coiled up in it and he likes to flick it around a bit which Dozzy says is why it might sound like a Gun Going Off But It Isn't A Gun And He's Clever With It. When she's not looking I check for Marks and there haven't been any I can see so I suppose that's True. Dozzy says he's one of the GentleMen on her LovelyMen List who are the ones who have always been Helpful but when I told her some of the Men don't look Lovely or Gentle to me she said MikkiLove You've Got To Stop Worrying. She is probably RIGHT but I still find it hard To TRUST A Man.

Dozzy calls where we live The Venice Of Newcastle because of so many streets alongside where Throsby Creek and The Styx used to run in their Concrete Drains have been washed away and they are Canals now. Sometimes it does look pretty like the pictures of Venice you used to see in a Magazine or Movie but each time a shitStorm comes though with massive wind and waves more buildings collapse and stuff like the abandoned cars gets sucked to rust or rot away in the Water sometimes even drowned people which makes it less pretty. Dozzy says what's good is It Puts The Rich People Off Buying Places Around Here but it's put some of the GiRLs off too and a lot have moved over to Broadmeadow where the trains have to stop now because A Big Section Of The Tracks got washed away. It's too far for me to go but there's still A Strip in Isso some Clients even come by Boat there'll always be Wanting Men. So I keep going out on the NightStreets with my Backpack of Helpful Things bandaids and bandages and antiseptic and arnica for Bruising plus the Biscuit Tin when Dozzy gives me money for ingredients and I can find sometimes just flour and sugar with an egg or oil that's been My Job a long time now I haven't done Proper Work since my injury because some People don't understand how I speak and I talk to myself when I forget things I never forget to look after Dozzy though and I never forgot to look after my daughter Bee when she came back to me after Welfare took her away. She still calls herself that Kidname Bee even now she's Boss of The Refuge where we used to stay she won't use the name her dad gave her After What He Did to me when she was Little.

He's one of The Roaches. Bee's dad. When I first heard He was Out Of Jail Again I was scared and Kept Watch but a few weeks back I was under a Street Light patching the face of a WraithKid who'd tried maybe to become a RoachKid or even a KidGiRL and copped a punch, and He appeared from the Edge of the Dark. He didn't come close but the Street Light made Him look like a monster still muscley but a bit bent over and black shadows instead of eyes and the WraithKid ran off half-patched without even a biscuit. I yelled at him I Don't Care What You Do To Me Just Get On With It but He said he would Look Out For Me so I yelled back Why Would I Believe It's Too Late To Change and he said Maybe Not Yet and went Back to the Dark. I knew it wouldn't be True but three Nights later someone came behind me on My Deaf Side so I didn't hear in time and yanked my Hair back hard so I couldn't move and said Give Me Money and I said I Don't Carry but they ripped my Backpack off and ran and I saw it was the WraithKid. She Came Back her face white because Bee's dad was Hauling Her Hard by the arm. She threw the Backpack at me and when I grabbed it I saw my Biscuit Tin was gone then both of them were too.

I was still crying when I got home so Dozzy came Down and I said GiRLs And Wraiths Even Roaches I'll Help But There Are More And More Roaches What If They Take The BOX From Us? Dozzy sat beside me on my sofa and massaged my lumpy head with her fingers the way she sometimes does and said Newcastle Still Has A Heart, MiKKI Love, We Have To Believe In That. And after a minute she laughed and said, Who's Going To Want A Cramped Old Signal Box Full Of Levers And Switches When There Are Entire Houses To Fight Over In The High Parts Of The City?

She had to go then because a LovelyMan was coming so I helped her up back Upstairs and when he came I saw through the curtain it was WhipMan.

There were a lot of gun sounds before I heard The Siren sound that Dozzy calls her Signal For When The Train Pulls Into The Station.

But everyone knows the Trains don't come here anymore.

Acknowledgements

I have situated the *Fig* story cycle in the *Coquun*/Hunter River valley and adjoining catchments. These are the lands of the Awabakal, Wonnarua and Worimi people. I am grateful for the stories and understanding of place and connection that they have shared, and recognise that the sovereignty of their lands was never ceded. Australia always was and always will be Aboriginal land.

I owe a debt of gratitude to my PhD supervisors Michael Sala, Hugh Craig, and Keri Glastonbury for their guidance and support in writing these stories, and for their patience and encouragement as my life veered in un-anticipatable directions.

My family has scaffolded this undertaking with the emotional and physical support I needed to complete. They have been my brains trust, technical and literary advisors, and astute editors. Thank you, Rick, Ned and Pippa Haughton and Hannah Stenstrom. I could not have done this without you.

Similarly, the *Fig* story cycle would not have come to fruition without the wisdom, suggestions and unflinching critiques of friends and fellow writers Julie Chevalier, Joanna Atherfold Finn, David Musgrave, David Kelly, Ed Wright, Linda Godfrey, Bronwyn Mehan, Morgan Bell, Trisha Pendergast and Judith Merrett. My understanding of Newcastle and its narratives was greatly expanded by my discussions with Zeny Giles, Brian Joyce, Paul Walsh, Ryan O'Neill, Ross Edmonds, Jude Conway, Lu Quade, the late John O'Donoghue and the late Vera Deacon, and Joanne McCarthy for her work in exposing the extensive abuse of children by Churches in the region covered in this book.

Thank you all.

About the Author

The lands of Mulubinba/Newcastle and the Coquun/Hunter River offer rich pickings for a writer, but those pickings are bittersweet. The region's history includes a brutal convict colony, displacement of First Nations peoples, a century of pollution and worker exploitation by the industrial monolith BHP, and horrific abuse of children by the Church. The beauty and deep spirituality of its mountain-to-coast landscape continues to be marred by evisceration for coal. Despite this the region is widely recognised for creativity and innovation in the arts, music, and literature, and the enriching cultural influences of the region's First Nations, migrant, queer, and otherwise diverse commnities. There is a potent connection to place here, and a community ready to fight to protect it, and the planet.

Dael Allison has been a fringe dweller of Newcastle for most of her life. She fell in love with the city on her first visit in the early seventies, which exposed her to her first plumber's crack rising above the waistband of a grubby pair of stubbies—apparently the one article of clothing (beyond a weary pair of thongs) its owner was wearing as he wandered laconically along Hunter Street. That fortifying and egalitarian image, along with her love for regional writing, has led to the stories in this book, all of which are based in real locations and on (mostly) real events.

Dael is a prize-winning poet, essayist and artist. Her Master of Creative Arts from the University of Technology, Sydney explored in poetry the life and art of modernist painter Ian Fairweather. Her Ph.D. from the University of Newcastle researched published narratives of the Coquun/Hunter region. Through these she traced responses to place in First Nations stories and physical texts, narratives from the convict era, colonial and industrial eras, and representations by contemporary writers.

That understanding of place helped colour *Fig*, her first publication of fiction.

www.ingramcontent.com/pod-product-compliance
Lightning Source LLC
La Vergne TN
LVHW090946080826
845145LV00003B/902

* 9 7 8 1 9 2 3 0 9 9 8 5 2 *